CO-AUG-566

Compliments of
HALF-PRICE BOOKS
CASTLETON· 577-0410

2.50
9 2 ω I X

Book # 828
B 21

The Mother
of the Graduate

By Cynthia Propper Seton

I THINK ROME IS BURNING
A SPECIAL AND CURIOUS BLESSING
THE MOTHER OF THE GRADUATE

The
MOTHER
of the
GRADUATE

Cynthia Propper Seton

 W · W · NORTON & COMPANY · INC ·
NEW YORK

COPYRIGHT © 1970 BY CYNTHIA PROPPER SETON

SBN   393   08612   7

Library of Congress Catalog Card No. 70-116111

ALL RIGHTS RESERVED
Published simultaneously in Canada
by George J. McLeod Limited, Toronto

PRINTED IN THE UNITED STATES OF AMERICA

2 3 4 5 6 7 8 9 0

For Lawrence K. Miller, editor of the *Berkshire Eagle*,
who started me

And for Tony,
who nearly finished me.

Contents

The Mother
of the Graduate

I Quiddities

> *Oh, do not ask, "What is it?"*
> *Let us go and make our visit.*
>
> T. S. ELIOT

I went to *The Graduate* because of the children who did not say, "Mother, you must see that movie." No, but for the few weeks that it was playing around this town they seemed to dip in for renewal (and for untold sums) and dip out with superior intelligence marked upon the brow which I doubted. By this unnerving ploy I was driven to see it and came out somewhat defensive, thinking about those children and how inflammable of them it was to pretend to see *us* trapped and captured by that silly plot. I was preparing to take a wide swing at it when my dear friend and oldest movie companion, his face all joyous smiles, chortled, "Absolutely marvelous, wasn't it?" Crocodile smiles brought about by nostalgia, as it turns out.

So there I was in yet another minority. I did like the movie, but I couldn't identify with anybody but the mother of the graduate, or more precisely, the wit's-endedness of the mother of the graduate. I couldn't see myself as the girl's mother because underneath all the nobler reasons, I like older men. There are people in America who did not see *The Graduate* and even some who may never have heard of *her* mother, and

I love them for it. Nothing that follows will be less intelligible on that account, because I see that in the end I only borrowed a few members of the cast for my occasional private use. In this instance it is Mrs. Robinson, *her* mother, a woman of my age who pursues and brings to bed the young hero of the title out of a simple but I guess fierce lust, something I found short of verisimilitude.

"Everything was so improbable," I explained, a little huffy about my friend's enthusiasm. "I mean women like her mother have no reality." And he explained, "*Oh* yes, they have," and went on to tell me about his encounter with one when he was just out of boyhood, and he was very far from regretting the whole shocking business, and in fact it was wonderful how philosophical we both became over Mrs. Robinson, who is about as kindly and sympathetic a character as Iago.

For a long time after I saw that movie I caught myself shadow-boxing with it, defending mothers and even marriage, and my clincher, as I visualized the last scene where the boy and girl ride out of wedlock off to their future in the back of a bus was, "All right. All right. Now you've got about fifty more years to live through. Now what are you going to do?" And I saw the re-entry of all the bourgeois, middle class, banal problems that nip at the heels of the rest of us.

At first I thought that if I wrote a book called *The Mother of the Graduate* it would be a magnificent testimony to me and my kind, self-serving perhaps, but who else in this youth-besotted world would serve us—we who are endlessly harried by the absurd tensions of middle-class parenthood and end-lessly undermined by melting tenderness, and *Who Did Not Walk Out!* I was once flipping through a movie magazine left behind in a summer house we rent at Kitty Hawk when my attention was fixed by a paragraph on Beautiful People who dyed their hair. It was a heartfelt sympathetic list of names, winding up with, "Yes, even Jackie Kennedy [that was] has some grey hairs, and who is more entitled?" With this touch of belligerence or defensiveness in tone, I would perhaps write a book about the younger generation, approaching as a partisan the question of wisdom of age.

But in order to write it, I thought, in all honor, I would have to see the movie again, which I *couldn't* do. I leave it mostly behind, now dim in my mind, but with thanks for the title I lifted from its context to put into mine, and for the initial stimulus it provided me. It certainly did act like a poke from a cattle prod into my private herd of irritations that generally chew their cud quiescent inside my rib cage. This ease with which any one of my (older) young seemed able to identify with the hero and heroine, their airy-fairy pose, from which we were to infer that Benjamin and his girl responded to precisely the intolerably materialistic conditions they themselves considered fleeing, it made me drum my fingers righteously, and who was more entitled? And I was impatient with the piteous cringing of my peers, of otherwise intelligent parents before the criticism of their radicalized sons and daughters. I thought our side must tighten up, must quit flopping down before just any indictment of our character and crimes. And indeed I did begin with the intention to rally our side, those over thirty, to wrest responsibility from the young, to assume a kind of progressive leadership in the righting of social wrongs, and I based my argument really on the belief that the difference between them and us was that they were immature and we were mature, but that we were hamstrung by guilt and sentimentality, and they drew their strength from the nearly biological righteousness of their age group. I was derisive. I mocked them and I mocked us. I called our side roughly anybody over thirty, and I understood that some members of the new generation actually themselves refused to accept the feasibility of proceeding beyond the age of 29, and I thought, Fine. Don't. It seemed to me then, and it seems to me now, that we, those on our side with the accrued wisdom, who hate The War, racial injustice, pollution, littering, False Values, ought to lead, not follow. We experience at least as much personal despair over American military adventures and brutal policemen as do our children. Why should we weep for their lot? We are more poignant, knowing more about the intractability of human illusions, and we don't weep for ourselves. Why should we weep for them? They need to be toughened, not pitied.

I drew, in the first chapter, the dimensions of my fixed position, and then in the chapters that followed I began slowly to move in on it, and I fragmented it. "You know," says Jean Renoir, "I believe one has to have only a rough idea where one is going when one is making a film or writing a story, or whatever—a rough scheme, like a salmon going upstream. No more than that." This is true. I find that when my own preconceptions are in control of an idea they seem often to be the deadening force, and when they let go of my mind I experience something analogous to taking the way of a salmon and am moved by the momentum, the vitality, of forces external to my preconceptions. This first chapter was thesis and it was my plan that the rest would be two hundred pages of explication. But, like a salmon, I went upstream and disordered the thesis, disregarded it. It has not become antithesis, nothing so neat.

I began with myself as parent, with a murmur of sympathy for the parents of Benjamin the graduate. It wasn't their tastes I shared, but their irritation and impatience. I don't even know anybody with their tastes, but I know lots of bright young people who are contemptuous of climbing to the top and collecting en route the baubles, like Jaguars and swimming pools; and to a boy, to a girl, they come from families where the mother has the kind of checkered career in which she was precinct captain for the McCarthy for President movement, and after that job folded she filled in her time with the committee to integrate the school system until she joined the tutorial for culturally deprived children, and the father works, reads, provides, and goes to bed. This college town is kind to people who live by humanist values, who rear their children by them. It is too easy to do. I am humbled sometimes by how easy it is. It seems to me irrational that we should blame ourselves for an American materialism so uncharacteristic of us, not to say difficult to achieve on our salary scale.

There is a tendency among this kind of people, the kind I am, to misspend our energies. The emotion flows, the mind goes. The very mother who has been collecting door to door for the Martin Luther King Fund, frantic over her 16-year-old son who is meanwhile smoking pot in the public park while declaiming against the racist society, is the woman who accepts the guilt for the violence and racism she abhors, accepts responsibility for gross tastes she doesn't have. It is as if she might logically assault her conscience and sigh, "Alas, what can I expect, what with Dad passing out Bloody Marys in his Hawaiian swimming costume by our Olympic-sized pool to our upper-echelon friends, some of whose wives may very likely pop off into their convertibles to meet boys young enough to be their sons in the beds of large expensive hotels?"

Why, for goodness sake, are we beating our breasts over the Graduate? Who are we to make personal amends for, of all American mothers' sons, Benjamin? Who are we? Benjamin, we see, is a sensitive, intelligent boy who rejects the gross values of his parents, while groping for the fine subtle ones discerned by his own fine subtle mind: the classic situation. But our children, and most of the children I know, espouse those same fine subtle values which they share with their fathers and mothers from whom they learned them. That is who we are. They've learned them from us, and they are implementing them. These catalytic times have invited them to move beyond our ethical posture, which was sincere, quite nicely integrated, statuesque, inert—move from inertia to its farthest cry, to a savage activation of every element in the body of our ethics.

I haven't believed for a long time that the elements of ethics, of morality, are disintegrating—although we may lose a few—so much as that they are in the process of regrouping. I never doubted that most furious students were ethically motivated, were charged by the most exalted ethical energy; every muscle tense, as it seemed to me, would have to be their condition to pass a resisting dean over their heads and down the stairs of a university building.

I, mother of the graduate, am tied by blood *and* by values

to the students on the barricades, but I counseled myself, my kind, to maintain a distance, not from ethical and political problems, but from our children. I thought we ought to strain our ties a little, pull away from an over-neat identification with 20-year-old university students, close ranks and bring our maturity, wisdom, money, influence, tact, and humor to bear upon *our* conceptions for the immediate reformation of society. My original thesis intended to be a circling around the subject of separation. I looked across what was called the generation gap and I saw mothers scrambling over helter-skelter, clutching clean laundry and homemade brownies, and I thought they should stop and consider whether this was wise.

Benjamin's family hovers uncertainly over its wayward son. Our families eschew uncertainty. When I read about the parents of balking students at the Sorbonne or Columbia, I didn't notice the mention of any unlocatable mother who couldn't be informed by the police of her son's imprisonment because she was spending the night in a motel with his apolitical roommate. All the mothers I read about were agonzing over their poor boys and sending them hot coffee and sandwiches while they held their buildings. Talk about the classic situation.

Or take Regis Debray. Surely he may be said to be first among the youngest, handsomest heroes of outraged students the world over, now serving his thirty years in a Bolivian jail for revolutionary activity. It is a heart-breaking waste—I speak both as a mother and as a not-uncritical political sympathizer. Well, and what of his mother? Was young Regis driven out to the far left in revulsion against a narrow rightist

French bourgeois home, than which, for banality and meanness at their worst, there is no worse in the world, see Balzac? Not at all. Not at all. His parents are largesse itself, educated, and in regard to their son, extremely supportive, and in fact have done everything before and since his trial to ease his lot. They've even made arrangements, as I read in the *Times,* with a nearby restaurant to have his meals sent over to his cell every day with a nice bottle of wine.

If we are the parents of those in this new generation whose conscience has been early and intricately and successfully sensitized by us, it is to our credit and to the bounty of this country that they are angry, intelligent, unafraid: that they care. We are proud and we understand.

But I think we are felled by our understanding. Benjamin's parents didn't understand his disdain for the American Way of Life, but all the parents I know understand it: a lot of them overunderstand it. It might be said that this is an affliction of my species of mother. We understand incontinently. I suspect that it may be an excess of love and understanding, rather than a paucity, that drives a young man to seek relief from the tender ministrations of *maman,* even in jail, although I don't insist upon it. And in the case of young M. Debray it would seem in vain.

I am in the habit of following immoderately every violent protest, every eruption, every spasm in what may well be the death throes of Western civilization, as recorded daily by *The New York Times.* I am shocked, elated, dismayed, appalled, by the anguish of the young. There seem to be no useful precedents to guide the responses of the old. But if I acknowledged the terrible contradictions, the wild, contrary swaths this converging complex of revolutions was cutting into an aging, relatively simple, classically ethical mind like mine, did it follow that I was morally bound to allow myself to be radicalized way back here in this house where I do the dishes and the ironing and throw out notices from the PTA? It was a rhetorical question I put to myself, asking No for an answer. Since then I have written myself into an uneasy Yes. I am an aging radicalized woman, herself surprised at the turn this book has taken. Almost immediately I swung away from "What are they doing!" backwards to "Why didn't we?" I am an aging radicalized *liberal*—a word that is nearly an epithet now, and one would think I would scarcely care to be called it—but the fact is that no matter how far out I may have gone with this new generation, I traveled with my heritage, with the humanist values I am accustomed to call liberal, even if that is semantically wrong.

Of the young of the 60s E. H. Carr, the British historian, wrote, "The first step towards reform was to bring down with a crash, the whole existing system: the second step it was premature to discuss. They were in all things aggressive. The 40s seemed to them an almost antediluvian epoch." It was the *19th* century Carr was referring to, the *1*840s and the *1*860s. Imagine such a parallel. But parallels are misleading. Meanwhile I take this statement with its dismissal of the nostalgic impotent middle-aged liberal, grandiose in his impotence, and I read it selectively, as a woman past forty, and not as a girl of twenty, and I choose to see in the 60s a coincidental recurrence of a simplistic impoverished ideology thrown up by social tensions in which "the worst are full of passionate intensity," while on the other hand I read into the 40s evidence of the endurance of humanist values. Not too fair.

We can know few things with certainty, but age makes us know this to the bone, that the first step towards reform, to bring down with a crash the whole existing system, is an empty vain one, that no phoenix rises from those ashes. We know, we on our side, that there are no solutions, but only essays at amelioration. There is something here simply unbridgeable between age and youth, this one truth whose time comes slowly, later; there are no solutions. It is our wisdom. The young don't want their ethical questions to be complicated, nor their intellectual propositions to contain contradictions, and they resist hearing that they are and that they do. But it is for us to be adamant, to insist. I do believe in our wisdom, and I don't want to diminish the value of it as my appreciation waxes for the wisdom that the young seem prematurely to have come into. I don't want to curry favor, and my original worry in my original thesis remains—that our liberal understanding of their frustrations tends to shade off into complicity with what we know isn't true and won't work. I would have us tighten up.

I would have to tighten up. In the first place, who are we and who are they? I refer to The Young and elide all distinctions within the new generation—Benjamin, our own children, hippies, Smith girls we've known, even Smith boys this year, an assortment of unpoliticals, 14 splinter groups of SDS— this widest, richest variety of individuals is lumped and loved, or not loved, by me, by turns. What is it that distinguishes them, what are their essences, their quiddities? *Quid est?*

In the second place, I wouldn't have Benjamin stand in

for them. Yes, it is a vacant, silly, boring rich society, and he cuts out. But he is at the bottom of the admirability scale, for all that he has the courage to leave, if courage it was. I began with Benjamin, wondering what he was going to do for the next fifty years, but I think I can guess. I drop him for a while now to pursue young people at the upper end of that scale. And I have pursued myself. For who am I to do it? I wandered into this subject like the man whom their minstrel, Bob Dylan, sings about: middle aged, one of us, who goes to a party, one of theirs, and hears the refrain, "Something is happening here but you don't know what it is, do you, Mr. Jones." *Quid est?*

II The Under-Used Generation

Men, lions, eagles and partridges, horned deer, geese, spiders, silent fish that dwell in the water, starfishes and creatures which cannot be seen by the eye—all living things, all living things, having completed their cycle of sorrow, are extinct. . . .

CHEKHOV

When my eye lit upon those words of Carr about the 40s and the 60s it was with the glee about irony that I slipped them out and pass them along. I don't subscribe to that genre of observation preserved by such remarks as History Repeats Itself, There is Nothing New Under the Sun. I do not believe history repeats itself and it has become my contention that everything is new under the sun, the new generation the most spectacularly new thing of all.

There are four girls growing up in our house, eight to sixteen now, but I don't know at what point in this past decade of revelations I absorbed into my view of them the fact that they were so infinitely more knowledgeable than I had been at their various ages that, as they grew towards womanhood, my own motherwit, my inherited tastes, judgments, values, and those wistful sorties into my own memory to try to recapture what they might be thinking and feeling—all this was not particularly handy.

About a year or so ago I heard myself rise up and announce to a group of women discussing the question of coeducation at Smith College that today's entering freshmen are a different breed of woman from what we were, that they were already en route to becoming such a substantially altered adult by the time they were in their first year of high school that they might better be approached with the hesitation, the diffidence one feels towards students from a foreign culture. I was surprised to hear me say this.

I went over to the college recently to a lecture by René Dubos, the biochemist—dragooned was I by an insistent friend ("He's fascinating. I read two of his books in a row and I couldn't put them down.") At lectures I have a short attention span which is growing shorter, and I dropped science in eighth grade for good, and I looked forward grimly to being very restless while being too old to knit and too old to wriggle. By too old I mean that it is unseemly in my position to bring my knitting as though it were the only way I could get through the time with some measure of contentment. It is usually the only way. Dr. Dubos, however, was not in that strange land, the other of the two cultures, Science, but seemed to have discovered in his biochemistry scientific confirmation of the humanist view. The young, Smith girls and the boys from Amherst and UMass, wriggled because they don't have to find in the gene pool the variety of things we need to find: the justification for being against littering *and* napalm. The older people from the faculty and the town drew the kind of spiritual comfort that our undoubting ancestors must have had from an uplifting sermon.

Specifically it was just a small statistic that lodged in my mind as regards this subject of altered women, and concerned the question of whether one would be entitled to think that the change was not simply quantitative, but had metamorphosed, figuratively speaking, from physical to chemical. Dr. Dubos was making the point that our environment had so radically and swiftly altered that in the United States alone the age of female maturation, which is now about twelve, was sixteen only a hundred years ago. The traditional institutional structures in which we lived (family, schools, church, state) meanwhile, evolving as they have through historical time, remained based upon such fixed biological truths as that maturation began at sixteen, a fact that is evidently not fixed, no longer true, but still determines our expectations.

That Dr. Dubos straddled science and humanity, and could readily move from genetics to Camus and James Baldwin was heartening, but if I look outward from Camus and Baldwin, it is over a vast divide, beyond which is a vaster and embracing ignorance, a moonscape where I keep Science and permanently store subjects like the military-industrial complex (bad) and the genetic code (good?), calories (bad) and pollution (terrible). It is probably science's claim to neutrality that I cannot recognize, accustomed as I am to keeping my environment tame and manageable by placing moral evaluations on everything in it.

Now just a few years ago I had found such phrases as "children mature earlier nowadays" irritating, and even went on to deride the idea in an article for *McCall's,* finding it ridiculously unDarwinian. My reasoning went this way, that given the lengthening of average life expectance and the increasing sophistication of the terms upon which one lived in civilization, why should the portion of life assigned for preparation grow shorter? Would not the evolutionary process be acting irresponsibly? It seemed to me then that because a boy of 16 could drive a car out of community supervision, and father a child, the credit ought to go to the advance in technology that made a car so simple to drive, and not to earlier human maturation, or even competence, and certainly not to the better judgment of our lad.

I had it all wrong, I think. What I did was impose my sense of order, which was then a kind of simple linear system of blocking out units of time in the life span suitable, or what I considered suitable for, for instance, maturing in at the front end of it, and being wise at the other. I haven't relinquished this linear progression altogether, but I have allowed to be introduced into my head so many more data of a three-dimensional and even four-dimensional complexity, that I find myself worrying, fiddling, picking over the pieces that will eventually prove to be the shape of the newest of the human species, and over why he is that shape, much in the way that James Watson worried at all the atoms and their properties that would have to fit congenially into the structure of DNA, whatever that is. In the end, everything must be accounted for.

Right through to the time that I heard Dr. Dubos I was unable to reconcile the need of today's human being for a longer adolescence through which to learn to cope with the unmatched complexity of life, with the fact that Tony and those four girls were in front of my eyes growing not just intellectually faster, but being wiser and readier for nearly everything much sooner than I allowed for. I did not like to call that Maturing Earlier. After Dubos, I was able to distinguish biological from genetic evolution. Technology, diet, medical knowledge could change our biological rhythm, and it has. And so the current biological rhythm of the human organism is in constant interchange with the rules, laws, and expectations of a social environment designed through history for the human organism before its rhythm changed. There results a sort of total cultural dislocation wherein a child grows at its own ineluctable rate while its elders, unconscious of any discrepancy, plan to receive him and mold him and instruct him at every point several years too late.

It's as if this notable *enfant terrible* were expected to arrive at Southampton, England, from New York on the *Queen Mary,* and delegates from all of Western Europe went down on the boat train to meet him and rolled out the wine-colored carpet by the wine-dark sea, and brought English flowers to the pier and at the appointed time, doffed their hats, and had the band play "God Save the Queen" and held out their hands, not taking into account that there isn't any *Queen Mary* any more, and that he plainly wasn't coming off it, having landed by jet last week and been in swinging London ever since.

Now if my object is to establish today's young as of a human quality historically unique, it was a boon to receive this underpinning from biochemistry. It had been absolutely outside my understanding of physiology that large biological responses could so swiftly be affected by new environmental stimuli. The illustration given me in school about evolution concerned toenails. Man was en route from having talons to sloughing off nails entirely, since he didn't need them any more for clawing up and down trees and in a few billion years they'd be gone. Quite opposed to this nail's pace was Dr. Dubos' information about the remarkably rapid adaptation of the body in the matter of maturation, and over this I mused amazedly for awhile. But then I saw that, remarkable as this swiftness was, it was not swift enough. If I am to account for the greatly expanded human beings my son and daughters are, compared to what I was, I would have to get rid of the fact that I matured in the neighborhood of twelve too, and more awkward still, so did my mother. This brings us back towards 1900, a round figure.

Why, if I were biologically all set to go, didn't I? Why the time lag? Why did *we* not burst outward; rupture the bonds of insensitivity; break the tradition of family ties, the moral rules of the church, the laws of the state; bring it all down, the lies and the truth, the good and the bad? Well, there are reasons innumerable why, and they pelt the brain, but look at it the other way round, and accept for the moment as fact that the finest of our young are matchless, without parallel in the breadth of their intellectual and moral comprehension, literally a new breed, see it as a beautiful leap to a higher human plateau, then ask the question why *they?* Why *now?* Then the answer must be rooted in what happened to us. They were nurtured by parents who were formed in the 20s, 30s, 40s; and when I try to pick us out of the past we seem two-dimensional, paper-thin by comparison. We seem formed by the relics of previous beliefs about God and responsibility and reason and virtue. The tendency was to constrain us so artificially by so narrow a mythical world view that the disparity between what we were capable of seeing and what we were permitted to see left our minds and sensibilities grossly uninstructed and under-used. We were the guests of Proteus and were stretched beyond what we could bear, and we snapped. These are the parents.

If I look back now and see what we were, from our childhood through our adolescence and into our marriage and parenthood, then I see us as a people destined to be miserably unbalanced, and I will take no joy in documenting the pain, but I do think it is instructive, and amusing, to see how we were gulled, how witless was the gulling, and how helpless we were as victims.

When I say "they" meaning this new breed, I would not like to wrap them into one woolly whole, because individual variations are enormous and a dismaying proportion of them seems to be miserably unbalanced, too. It would have to be so. It is always the case in nature that a generation of vipers can be produced only by progenitors who are vipers themselves. But this is too nasty a slur on the processes of generation in civilization, and in fact a remarkable characteristic of our times is that, given the degree of emotional wretchedness, so little of it is the consequence of people's being vicious and predatory.

When I refer to the young it will usually mean this new breed, a small part of the whole. They are a phenomenon arriving in the 60s in all the colors and sexes. A distinguishing group characteristic concerns discrepancy: they have no tolerance for it, for our brand of it. They won't live with it.

Our brand of discrepancy between word and deed, between

what we valued and what we said we valued was so threaded through the fabrication of the reality we knew, that although *now,* while we might look back upon the pattern of our beliefs and be astonished at how naive we were not to see the pockmark of flaws, *then* we regarded as naive any serious efforts to bring deed into closer correspondence with word.

There is a pack of letters on my desk, part laudatory, part furious, responding to an article I wrote about the permissive society and the rearing of young girls in it, and there was a phrase used by an angry woman that I will borrow in order to illustrate "discrepancy." My correspondent chastised and admonished me through a paragraph that ended, "It is God's will that a woman preserve her body as a precious gift for her husband." In earlier times, before World War I, before we were cut loose from our moorings, you could say this and believe this, and be at peace with it, furthermore, it not falling into the category of an idea exposed to jostling in the market place. There was no discrepancy. From about 1920 to 1960, in those forty years, you might affirm it if pressured to take a stand, meanwhile not believing it. Discrepancy. Today, if you don't believe it you don't say you believe it. No discrepancy.

I walked into the kitchen with this letter to try out the phrase on Julie and her friend, who are seniors in high school, and serious as was my delivery, I still expected they would giggle. But both girls looked up at me as if I had said something in Classical Greek and they didn't take that course. Blank. They never struggled, these young females, with the classification of Woman as opposed to Man, of woman as secondary or lesser, a creature needing to be liberated. They would never think of themselves as the Donor Sex, and they don't credit the fact that anybody else would think of them in that category either. No more does a butterfly think of himself as a caterpillar, I suppose.

But in regard to "We" and "They": I seem to let land masses of generalizations form around these two words so that they have continental contours, while my own ear for generalizations others make is as acute as for a split infinitive. I hear them as a challenge to really disbelieve. One talks about people in the lump, but the salient property of a lump of people is that it is friable. Dr. Dubos put the authority of science behind the assertion that every man born *whenever* is unique, unprecedented and unrepeatable, a natural phenomenon that the Good Cynthia reveres.

They, the young girls of sixteen to eighteen I know and admire, hearing it is God's will that a woman preserve her body as a precious gift for her husband, do not necessarily disbelieve in God, nor do they laugh at the notion of a gift. Each might give that proposition her personal consideration (or might not). They are very individual and they are very moral. Indeed, they must surely all believe that their destiny is to know a great love. And while they are still so particularly young, the most bountifully lovely and romantic vision of all is that *before* you find this love, you are an ordinary mundane self, the real potential untapped, but that upon the arrival of that great love the whole of you becomes transformed. It's not by God's will but by your own free will that you might plan to save yourself for this experience, to heighten it, to sanctify it. It is not a gift in the category of a dowry and a dot. But it may remain, to the romantic fancies of one kind of girl, her really sophisticated, independent, free, and undirected choice that she wait. It is not a gift. It is a point of view. They don't seem to be prey to the ancient necessity to converge on one point of view and call it moral. They seem born to a lovely latitude. They amble in this ambiance, this generous ambiance.

When I say *they,* when I try to distinguish their uniqueness, really what I am directing attention to is the enormously enlarged world-view in the process of being for better and for worse demythologized, in which they are growing; a world-view which invites, rather insistently invites, each young woman to keep her intentions and attitudes fluid, mobile, to allow for traveling light. Lightweight and superficial does this make them? Or does it keep them from being foolishly encumbered?

And when I say *we* I mean me. I am no sociologist. I am one of their digits, and I entertain no expectations that a few autobiographical reflections of a digit will alter the shape of their fine graphs. At this juncture in my argument I must eschew being spokesman for the whole living population of America, 1920–60, and instead suggest that my interaction with a larger world, with society, that began roughly when I was six, in 1932 and remained receptive and relatively uncritical for the next ten or twelve years, was the era that molded me for life. 1932–42 that was the decade that taught me to think, and ever afterwards I have had to struggle to unthink through that girl's eyes.

This is of course something different from Freud's ascribing to the first three years of life the nearly unalterable form of the personality and character of a human being. Dr. Dubos gives five years to this process but includes the nine months *in utero* and extends the psychological to the physiological. Give me a child for the first seven years, said Loyola, and the world can have him after.

I intend only to identify a kind of basic girl self with whom *consciously* I parry. She accounts for curious oddments such as the fact that while I circled at the edge of a student protest meeting one easy mild spring night, subscribing to the substance of their Demands, overcoming even more or less a habit of choking on the lingo, I was crushed in an instant by hearing a girl's voice bawl out an obscenity to the speaker. It doesn't ruffle me that these girls pursue the most unconventional life styles, stand on picket lines, go to jail, sleep with whom they will, but I am suddenly sickened by a woman's voice yelling out a four-letter word I even use myself upon such occasions as letting a raw egg drop to the kitchen floor.

That four-letter word is the limit. It spells out the limit of what I can bear to see jettisoned of Western civilized values. This tradition includes the invigorating impulse on the part of youth to flout, *épater le bourgeois*. Thus do the boys shock us with longer and longer hair, the girls with shorter and shorter skirts. We think it's not funny! But, really, it is funny, a lot of it is funny. A lot more of it is annoying, or unseemly. But for me there is a limit in the kind of discourtesy that shrivels the other person, that forecloses reconciliation, forgiving, and forgetting. The young, some of the young, cruelly underprize courtesy.

III Across the River and into the Revolutions

I must remark that the culture of which I talked was an endeavor to come at reason and the will of God by means of reading, observing, and thinking; and that whoever calls anything else culture, may, indeed, call it so if he likes, but then he talks of something quite different from what I talked of.

MATTHEW ARNOLD

The Connecticut River, claimed by local boosters to be the world's most beautifully landscaped sewer, is spanned by the Calvin Coolidge Bridge. Stretching out east and west of it for a few miles is a densely cultured population serving four-going-on-five institutions of higher learning from which weekly bulletins are issued inviting the public to an unbelievably rich assortment of events. We are immensely stimulated by living here, although the number of things we attend each week comes down to roughly none. We, the parents. Our children think of themselves as the Audience for whom all this is mounted. And I do their mother and father a disservice. A truer picture would have us off in a flurry to three of four lectures in October or March and then subsiding for a long time, happy in the dual comfort of feeling surrounded by so much good fortune, and not drawing upon it. At this writing it is a period of subsidence, but I am remembering one other lecture I attended years ago through which neither did I knit, nor did I wriggle once. It was on Janus, the two-faced Italian deity (from which, of course, *January*), whom *The Oxford Companion to English Literature* identifies as a god of door-ways. He was also the god of river-crossings, as it was explained by Louise Holland, the archeologist. I am best able to explain the spell Mrs. Holland wrought on my imagination by saying that I'm left with the impressionist dream that she and her husband passed their whole life together again and again fanning outward on foot from one of the seven hills of Rome, first having cleared off all traces of all civilizations, walking over the fields and under the forests of pre-history, until they were delayed by the need to cross a stream, or stopped by the impossibility of crossing a racing river. For years and years they arrived at the edges of racing rivers, and it seemed to me a wonderful thing to arrive at, I, who walk from the house door to the car door, and at the utmost, from the car door to the door of a jet plane, never once coming upon Janus, god of doorways.

They wandered over every foot of tribal land through that era before the art of bridge-building, when a good-sized river like the Connecticut was most of the year unfordable, and the people on either bank were without connection to each other, entirely separate, alien, independent, suspicious, fearful, as though on the left could evolve the small-brained Dinosauria and on the right the fleet-footed Herbivora. I have ever since noticed the flow of rivers through history, myth, and literature, the wealth of meaning they contain, the banks as boundaries, impasses, as the edges of existence, nearly nobody crossing over—but always somebody having to risk everything, obeying an inner compulsion to get to the other side—and the singular, often sacred calling of the ferryman, the man who is the bridge before there are bridges. Mrs. Holland would find the place where the crossing must have been by the remains of a stone statue of Janus, god of river crossings, the god who looked upon his own people, and looked upon alien, unknown, feared people, equally.

Now, I bring this up in order to pontificate upon the virtually unbridgeable. A great river, current-driven, rushing to the sea took such purchase on the imagination because there was no bridge, because there was the finality of the banks of it; because some irrepressible souls needed to get across notwithstanding; because the ferryman was sanctified; because this natural barrier almost totally separated man from man, almost totally alienated him from his fellow; and because this separation, this alienation could be effected just as neatly without any river at all to divide them.

I'd rather have a great river represent the division between our alienated generations, because I'm tired of gaps, and water is regenerative and buoyant. I like the image of a river because it contains the *necessity* of a crossing, presided over by a two-faced god who looks upon each circular, self-congratulatory, exclusory generation with composure. I warm to ancient evidence that there are always some strays to make the crossing, to be the bridge, to pontificate (from *pons, pontis: bridge,* to *pontiff: bridgefinder, pathfinder, waymaker,* —a derivation noted in an essay in *The New Republic*). It would be easy for me to pontificate upon the sluggish, indolent way our tribe of elders has remained insensible to the fact that our young are ready for adult responsibility years before the magic age of twenty-one.

What would have happened if, say, at the end of World War II the whole legal apparatus of adulthood had been lowered from twenty-one to eighteen? It would have meant that, were you a restless, bright, critical sixteen, you would have been within reasonable proximity to the coming of age, to full citizenship, to the saving of the world through constitutional means, by rational discourse, in the democratic tradition. Instead our restless, bright, critical children were prepared to move from early adolescence into a vacuum, and they abhorred it, naturally. And then out of the blue, it seems, they made their own self-sufficient culture, left our Democracy, constructed for themselves a Relevancy, refusing to inherit our discrepancies, distrusting rational discourse, constitutional means, and other refinements of civilization, refinements they wrongly despise, I believe. And they smoke pot. Would there have evolved a separated culture, alienated from ours, a drug culture, if the legal drinking age as well as the age of enfranchisement had dropped to eighteen? Smug they are with their own society and their own dress and their own ethics and their own pastimes, and we are furious that they won't, instead, spend the years from sixteen to twenty-one marking time.

Abruptly it has come to this, that there are two antipathetic cultures, and a great natural barrier (which you can see as a wide swift river or as the human mind) keeps them antipathetic in the primordial manner. And I am my own witness how easily I thought of their tribe with hostility (What they look like! The language they use! Their morals!) once I caught on to the idea that it might exist, this tribe, indeed be flourishing, on the other side; and this is the more remarkable, since I really didn't know a member of it. Only in the last few years have our own children, still under twenty, broadened our lives with their friendships and associations. Of the older young, those from twenty to thirty who are the activists, the idea people, few live representatives had crossed the path of my mind until one settled into the couch of our living room, brought by Maggie, and had to say several times to me, as I stumbled along the small openings to conversation with "Have you read . . . ?" "I don't read." Well, I thought, here is my first McLuhan man. He really means he doesn't read. And this would not have been so odd to me had he not been a candidate for a Ph.D, spending his year in the Northampton School system to support himself while filming his thesis. He is taking this doctorate in the movies.

We loved him. He was wonderful, alert, engaging, intelligent, with a startling sensitivity, an extrasensitivity possibly (I explain to myself) that non-literates develop the way the sense of touch and sound in blind people become more acute in order to compensate. But the blind have braille and "talking books" and so they can "read," and those who do read may experience a growth in themselves that can only come through the printed word. That you have to read is the only absolute I have left.

We were waiting for Maggie, he and I, and so to put me at my ease and in the most graceful way, he guided me along my own hallway to look at the pictures we have hanging, and then he had us pause so that he could read the calligraphy beneath an etching of Sacco and Vanzetti by Ben Shahn. ("If it had not been for these thing, I have live out my life talking at street corners to scorning men. . . .")

"Who are they?"

"Sacco and Vanzetti."

"I might have seen the movie but I didn't read the book. I told you I don't read."

Well, if it comes to that, you know, I didn't read the book either.

Actually we had had one encounter before, he and I, although we didn't refer to it. It was early in the fall, when he couldn't have been in town more than a few weeks, but when he had already won the loyalty until death of all the students at Hawley Junior High. Maggie plays the bass clarinet for the school band, probably her only failing; and as it is a very heavy instrument that she absolutely must have in school on the days when it is home and vice versa, I who have stalwartly and pretty successfully refused to be chauffeur to my children, and jolly car-pool participant, and things like that, find that I am driving that damned clarinet back and forth all the time. It was one Saturday morning that I met this man. He had unlocked the school door so that Maggie could run up, and there we were. But I didn't open up then with "Have you read. . . ." I said something like "How do you like Northampton?" And I don't apoligize for a remark like that, believing that not every encounter needs to initiate something memorable. Rest periods. I think much of rest periods.

However, when I said "How do you like Northampton?" he said—and I reconstruct the gist, "It is a very remote and protected place and none of you knows anything about what's going on in the world. If you're a teacher and you haven't taught kids in the ghetto then your perspective is useless, not real. You faculty families, you think you can sign a petition or stand in a vigil and you're real activists, but you don't know a thing about the nitty-gritty." Here he was, you know, pausing in the Connecticut Valley, looking across the great flow of our river where he saw us reading and writing, remote as ever from the living pain, the reeling and writhing.

I protested mildly with not much interest because I was wondering where Maggie was, and memorizing my grocery list—whipping cream, watercress, the *Times,* Captain Crunch for Nora—I even remember the list. (It is apposite to note here, were I to spell out the littleness in my nature [how beautifully impervious I am to the tiny inroads of Newspeak and Madison Ave. and the Communic. Rev.], I would spell it Captain Crunch.) That I am not impervious to the larger inroads will be evident.

Probably the sort of defense I made was based upon my Murmuring Modestly about writing for a newspaper, the role of ideas, the printed word, but I couldn't know then how unimpressed he'd likely be with those weapons, my fierce weapons. Whatever I said made him very angry and he delivered an indictment of me and my kind and wound up with, "You know what you are? You are an armchair liberal!" And that's when I fell. It was so divine to be that bad with that redolence, to be routed by the very words I had ineffectually spattered against my father's armor a quarter of a century before this revolution.

This revolution: in Webster's Second International dictionary, which is altogether pre-revolution, pre-McLuhan by definition, one might say, which has Values and makes Judgments, which is the unlikely and sometimes only comfort left to the self-measuring book-reading Remnant—in this Webster's they seem mostly interested in revolution as it applies to planets, and hardly at all as it applies to people, reserving for its seventh and last meaning not much more than that it is "a fundamental change in political organization." But on the facing page they have printed what they call a TABLE OF REVOLUTIONS IN MODERN TIMES (as of about 1934) and, obviously trying to be as fair as possible, they've listed in the left-hand column in alphabetical order almost every country, and given each at least one revolution. ("Spanish America" is a single entry). It's an interesting table with the other columns headed "Date." "Causes and Parties," "Main Events and Leaders," "Results."

The results are usually short-lived and disheartening, and this suggests to me that the most modern meaning of the word *revolution* had better go beyond "a fundamental change in political organization" to "a fundamental change in the way men regard themselves." In *The Ideological Origins of the American Revolution,* Bernard Bailyn suggests that the American Revolution occurred in the fifteen years before 1776. *Then* a change of perspective was effected in the minds of a significant body of American colonists, so that before what is called the Revolution began, it was already a *fait accompli*. The old reality in which allegiance to the mother country was supremely right had been replaced by the new reality in which "when tyranny is abroad, submission is a crime." So for our students today, the new ethic about war and race and sex is not something one argues for, defends. It is the bedrock upon which all of us as individuals, in which America itself, can alone be justified.

They have been born into this somehow. They haven't had to fight free of older, narrower conceptions of right and wrong, as the rest of us do and are. The fact that we have to fight at all is incomprehensible to them, and that we are so slow is intolerable, because in their minds the revolution is won; it's over, all but the bloodshed. This second American Revolution is of unassessable magnitude and difficult to date. It has causes, parties, main events, leaders, and results, but it's hard to say about dates. Each of us may have to choose his own.

The definition for this kind of revolution that occurs in a people's philosophy must include new characteristics: its consequences cannot be short-lived, for it isn't a question of having a new constitution revoked. It must be in some sense irreversible, because we aren't able to retreat backwards into a human understanding that knew less, into the New Deal world of right and wrong in which I grew up, inside which my father took his bearings until he died. But, of course, whether it plunges on or spends itself it can have the disheartening results.

There is a girl we know who is a senior at Smith this year, and is Our Girl on Campus, another great link with the "older young." She comes over on Wednesday evenings to teach Maggie and Nora the piano. We all admire her, long straight black-brown hair, black-brown eyes. Joanne looks solid and good and she is. I want to talk to her about Smith which she has assured me she *hates,* and so after dinner one night, and after lessons, we settle into the library, and I, ever needing to fend off small truths, having to numb in advance the pain I am inviting myself to suffer, I try to produce a more benevolent climate to our conversation by warming up the cause for my devotion to the college, and I inveigle her, I say a little guiltily now, to consider aspects of the college community which have transcending value (she concurs) that she had never thought of.

"Well, really I loved Smith, I *loved* it my freshman and sophomore years," she said in her warmest voice. "Now I hate it." Flat and cold. She might date the revolution by this, her own twentieth year, or Smith might.

At some unascertainable date, not marked by any particular cause, party, main event, leader, etc., one's feet are on new ground. Before, while the changes in perspective and belief were welling, were accumulating, one still marked one's place within the old framework of reference. Then, flipflop, the revolution is suddenly completed in your head, but not the details, not the color or the texture, and you might say your frame of reference is new, but it is perhaps more descriptive to say that your reference has not as yet a framework. You are like those first amphibious creatures who crawled up on the shore and decided to stay. You find that you are rethinking everything and many of your opinions would have to have appended to them Old Style. New Style like the calendar of Napoleonic events at the back of my copy of *War and Peace*.

I ask our Smith senior to talk because I want to keep communications open, but I say this with no particular anguish. I am just curious to see what is happening to them so that I can see what might happen to me. She and my own children as well are interacting with a radically different environment from the one that made me. It's as if I grew up still living mostly in the sea, continuing to find it more congenial to duck under the water and breath through my gills and chase minnows, while they are altogether creatures of the air, a somewhat vegetarian species already adapted to the land. They not only wouldn't go back to live under water, they couldn't.

Their environment is the open sky, full of free air, and this open sky has no top upon which to locate heaven and so there is no God directing affairs. The consequence seems to be, though I don't know that I could trace the intricate causes and effects, that their loves and loyalties, which they have in plenty, are not to God, Country, Smith, mother and father, to the *institutions* and the communities that are their birthright. Their loves and loyalties are free-floating and attach to selected individuals and to groups that are their creation. The very interesting moral point here is that they don't inherit our institutional vendettas. They aren't loyal to our loves and they aren't loyal to our hates. Love Smith Old Style and you are enmeshed in a community that has a history. To love Smith New Style might seem to rest upon the success of the plans to dismantle it.

"The most important thing is to communicate," says our beautiful piano player, telling me the truth, the key to the whole business. I see the whites of her eyes but I don't shoot. We use the very verb *communicate* in an uncommunicable way. When I say it, I mean that I like to watch what's going on with the young, what seeds they are sowing, because I have about thirty more years to plan for myself and they are surely the nurturers of my future environment as I have been of their past. I am looking for intellectual and ethical content in the ideas that come from them to me. They come because I reach for them. Meanwhile I am a Cultural Wellspring, a repository of their heritage, their tie to human history, a monument of worthy stolidity difficult to overlook, I would think. I would have thought. But were I by the wildest chance to fall into their line of vision, they would not reach for me except coolly to untie the tie.

For me, to communicate implies exchange, "rational discourse," talkers and listeners on each side. For her the most important thing is to communicate, one to one—"I care about you for what you are!"—in this teeming world where you would think we could manage our survival only by collecting in tidy aggregates, each with a leader speaking for ten million of one type of person or another. You do this by constitutional means, through the democratic process.

For her the barrier to communication, one to one, is community as we have known it, the nation, the town, the college, the family. In every sort of historical community the spontaneity of an individual is strapped down by irrelevant rules, his essence denatured by prescribed loyalty, a loyalty that is often swollen to exalted love of our own kind by our hot hate of others.

> "But man with man and state with state
> Shall vow *The pledge of common hate*
> *And common friendship*. . . ."

That is the prescription for successful human communities, for happy families, booster towns, top nations. That is how Aeschylus resolves the tragedy of the House of Atreus with its ghastly parricides, that is how he wishes Athens well for the future:

> "The thirsty dust shall nevermore
> Suck up the darkly streaming gore
> Of civic broils, shed out in wrath
> And vengeance, crying death for death!
> But man with man and state with state
> Shall vow *The pledge of common hate*
> *And common friendship. . . ."*

I let these two, our Smith girl and that doctor of the cinema, represent a little revolutionary cell in my brain, all the while remembering that The Young is not monolithic, but a shorthand term for that relatively small number of their generation that is bright and feeling—but not too small a number. Inside the term there are many mansions, and Joanne belongs to a musical subdivision which I suspect is composed of non-readers too. I have to warn her about the reading. It comes as a shock, when you are moving through your maturity, to find that people in the world of music can be non-literate, as if music were not embraced by the humanities.

She isn't disappointing now, although since she finds it galling to live in a dormitory governed by any rules, and therefore insists that salvation depends upon off-campus housing, she is effectively proposing to atomize the college community that I love. In fact she is admirable, intending to direct the full force of her belief in communication towards inspiring musical responses in ghetto children. But I detect an impatience with those girls at the college who are not primarily doers, activists, who do not burst with spontaneity, with essence undenatured, but who are still ponderers, musers, who can't communicate forthrightly with those black-brown eyes, but need to submerge themselves, retreat: who read.

"But you know," I say, defending the non-doers, "when they announced the three-day fast for peace, at least three quarters of the undergraduate students joined, and very soberly, and they all seem very straight about integration. . . ."

"Oh, Mrs. Seton," she said, in a tone that suggested I had brought up a point of the greatest irrelevance, "Everybody here is for peace and racial equality. That doesn't mean anything."

That doesn't mean anything? Why, that means that the revolution is accomplished. That could mean that they will renounce the pledge of common hate after the blood-letting.

IV   A Short Chapter
on Short Time

> *And indeed there will be time*
> *For the yellow smoke that slides along the street,*
> *Rubbing its back upon the window-panes;*
> *There will be time, there will be time*
> *To prepare a face to meet the faces that you meet;*
> *There will be time to murder and create,*
> *And time for all the works and days of hands*
> *That lift and drop a question on your plate;*
> *Time for you and time for me,*
> *And time yet for a hundred indecisions,*
> *And for a hundred visions and revisions,*
> *Before the taking of a toast and tea.*
>
>   *The Love Song of J. Alfred Prufrock*

And indeed, perhaps there won't be time. As I count them this morning in Northampton, there are three revolutions completing themselves in the American mind; the racial, the ethical, the sexual; and if they converge at this moment, it may be because we are threatened with the truncation of time; the prospect that time, for our human purposes, is about to be terminated.

It is only a very short while since educated people in significant numbers have ceased to believe in an afterlife. Darwin says of himself that he was at (spiritual) sea as a young man and went into the ministry *because* he had no calling (thought to be the better part of wisdom, that, in the nineteenth century) and that when he left to board the *Beagle* he was an unquestioning and unconflicted believer in the Thirty-nine Articles of the Church of England. Increasingly in our century and culture, man has had to relinquish the comfort of being *infinitely* of significance and settle for seventy-five years of significance, quite a cutting down, and no wonder one harbors some reluctance to give up heaven altogether.

I myself, who took the word *firmament* to mean *earth* until about twenty minutes ago on account of the solid sound of the first syllable and lifetime's neglect of religious instruction, I, yea, even I take metaphysical comfort from believing that our world is tucked safely into eternity; but it isn't. Is the end of time coming up? Are we all to be exterminated for ecological reasons or because we cannot control the consequences of our aggression? In the undisciplined, rude, uncompromising *demands* of political revolutionaries there are indeed echoes of past revolutions and past revolutionaries. What is a new fact, new reality, is the new given: No Time. And I think this new temporality is of primary moment in assessing the three revolutions, one new Given distinguishing Now from all human past. You can't look at a girl on the Smith campus today and try to guess what womanhood means to her, and marriage and love and sexuality, without remembering, from time to time, that time itself has lost its infinity.

I go to two meetings a year, and on Friday when I was walking out of one of them, a Smith alumna '03, wheeling herself in her wheelchair, looked up at me and said firmly, "These young people do not allow *time* for change," and she was indignant with the incivility, the impertinence of their very language that expresses their disdain for time, for the idea that waiting is a good thing. I, who am deeply conservative and traditional and middle-aged, and live privately and most happily in a nineteenth-century world, stirred by Matthew Arnold's desire to be clear about fundamentals before we proceed to reform, I believe—having brought myself to face the question—that there is no time. And I think about how it must be for a young woman under this cloud who would want to love someone to the end of time, and it doesn't seem long enough, could seem to diminish, might seem to make shabby the love she would want to give.

As to the clouds above our town, we have not yet had one mushroom-shaped, but occasionally, on still, windless days, there is a yellow smoke that slides along the street. This enlightened community burns its wastes in an open dump which sends effluvium up into the sky. In fact, you can pick out Northamptom from miles away by our dump smoke. Wonderful. We've been ordered by the state to stop. We have been brought to court. But no neighborhood in our county will allow part of itself to be used for a site for sanitary disposal. "Let's take the land from the Audubon Society," said a town councilor in a burst of creative thought. Over Smith there drifts this reminding climate. There is no time.

Or trail your finger idly from a boat on the Connecticut River and you're liable to pull out a bone, the flesh disintegrated. So much for the metaphor of cleansing and renewal. And this river flows through the most beautiful farmland, the Tobacco Valley; and have they stopped spraying the crops by air—tobacco, potatoes, onions, asparagus? If they have stopped, it will not have been because a local town council took the responsibility to issue a local ordinance. That would be political suicide. And you can't play tennis on the college courts when the wind is coming from the felt factory, but also you can't push the felt factory or it'll go to South Carolina. That would be community suicide. What we need is new industry, on account of the tax base, and we'll make any concessions. Great hopes rest upon the return of power from the federal government to the local community, but not my great hopes. We *will* not govern wisely, and there's not time to govern foolishly. "Men, lions, eagles and partridges, horned deer, geese, spiders, silent fish," certainly seem on the way to completing their cycle of sorrow around here. Lions, eagles, partridges, you can just count them out already. So in lieu of a willingness to volunteer ourselves for sacrifice, we have to settle for racial suicide.

For the girls at the college, however, there is a contradiction about time that contributes to the way they see themselves and the world. Taking their seventy-five years as sure, and allowing for where eventually their husbands will need them and when inevitably their children will need them (allowances some of them are thinking of not making, after all), they are still able to preserve to themselves great latitude for what they may want to do, whenever they may be ready to do it. This is new latitude. This was not the latitude I knew when I was at Smith. In my girl's eyes the lifeline of an adult female was notched in segments with a cleaver: You started with the degree. Then you got a job which was not to signify, not to have a future, not to tie you into some larger meaning, somebody else's plan, but to occupy those days of that first and shortest segment of time marked out for the purpose of Having Fun Before You Settle Down. Next you were to fall in love and marry, and your wedding night was to be the apex of all the human happiness allotted to you, chop goes the cleaver, and the long final segment is the post-fun settling down where you get your small satisfactions, catch as catch can, until the cleaver severs you from everything for good.

For almost every girl I knew, bright or dull, this was life's program. With the exceptions of those few who had a vocation and went on to professional training, there was no other program, no format, no scenario, too little in history and literature and tradition for one's fancy to draw upon to consider that a serious adventure could be made out of that long final segment.

For our girls, there's a whole life's worth of time for which to plan, the bounty, the consequence, and the reason for the sexual revolution. What is now becoming a fact was then for me an abstraction, a thesis I could have defended in a term paper, but which wasn't inside me to feel. To have said to me "All right. All right. You have about fifty more years to live through. Now what are you going to do?" would have been an alarm bell to all my defenses. My many fancy poses and advanced views notwithstanding, what else could I do but fall in love, get married, have children, live until I die?

But each of these girls gets fifty years as a gift nearly unentailed. If there are fifty years left of life on earth, that is, they're hers. And I think that this contradiction that inheres in the concept of time now produces in young women in particular the restlessness and depression and the flouting of wisdom and age: young women who by nature have always needed and would always need time for their devotion, and for their nurturing; these young women in whose minds the revolution has already taken place, whom it has already freed, have just as abruptly and as if it were part of the package been robbed of the promise of time.

V Tigers and Leopards

Her mind was theoretic, and yearned by its nature after
some lofty conception of the world which might frankly
include the parish of Tipton and her own rule of con-
duct there; she was enamoured of intensity and great-
ness, and rash in embracing whatever seemed to her to
have those aspects; likely to seek martyrdom, to make
retractations, and then to incur martyrdom after all in
a quarter where she had not sought it.

Middlemarch

It may be useful to bear in mind this matrix of the sense of
urgency when one considers how coeducation leapt from
being no issue at all to being a non-negotiable demand in
something like a day and a half. But were there not the
urgency there would still remain a good argument, as it came
to me when I was watching Princeton decide whether and
when to admit women.

While it was still in the air, the very idea of females in a
condition of legitimacy at the old alma mater stirred some
aging tigers who planned to snarl very fiercely at the trustees
because coeducation "would weaken the quality of education
and perhaps topple the institution's financial structure." The
man from the class of 1940 who led the unsuccessful insur-
rection is a living tribute to the intensity of nostalgia Old

Nassau evokes, if not to the growth of mind and vision it stimulates.

What probably really put him into a flap were the student demonstrations against the university's investment policies, and he was taking this stand on women as a punitive measure against naughty boys. He was not precisely against naughty boys, and in fact, when he was young—"Why, if I could tell you what goes on in Princeton dormitories . . . I better not go into that"—it wasn't financial structures you toppled, ho-ho-ho.

"In our time," I'm quoting from a news article in the *Times,* "a Princeton man had the reputation of being a dashing, undisciplined fellow." But, as the *Times* article had him explaining, such a reputation never conflicted with the university's old motto, "Princeton in the Nation's Service." But it seems to me unimaginative to presume that the position of women in Princeton in 1940 was nobler than their position in 1970. In 1940, it was left to be surmised, when the old Harry needed a woman he had a woman, and then, back to his "exclusive male collegiate society in which young men treasured the candor of dormitory bull sessions and the long, solitary hours of library study."

I do not, myself, dismiss the value of long solitary hours of study, nor the sweetness of privacy. I would like to have it both ways. And to borrow the candor of those dormitory bull sessions, those few which were not exclusively centered upon intellectual matters, I hear this as relishing the age-old male cleverness of managing your satisfaction with women without having them hanging on your neck all the time. I hear in that chortle a kind of awful moralizing about respect for that category of female reserved for use as mothers, sisters, wives of Princeton men; but I hear nothing about the other category assigned for the other use.

He undersells his generation, this tiger; he is a self-selected parody. Awkardly ill-defined as the going was then for the concept of equality, it was, I really believe, en route to being welcomed by the young men at Princeton and Amherst as a good thing, as an interesting move. I know them now—some —who have a profound feeling for this change in the way women see themselves and who regret that the women they loved and married came along too early to be at peace with it. I came along too early, too.

By tracking down that old tiger to his undergraduate stamping grounds, by tracking myself back to Smith in the class of 1948, I wonder if I can surprise us in that pristine state of not yet knowing. Not Yet Knowing. If I were able to make our younger selves clear as we walked through those remote campuses in that remote world, creatures still unaware that doom impended, could I make understandable and reasonable why suddenly it seems necessary to include women at Princeton and Amherst, to include men at Smith; why, in the eyes of the young, it is part of the rectification of our massive cultural dislocation?

Do you think it is a fad? It is true that students around here are dappled with whims and fads like leopards in the jungle, and for a while it was easy enough to make the case for saying there's nothing there, it's all shadows and lights. All this blowing up of coeducation is merely the production of a numerically insignificant claque of students with an unholy capacity about decibels, wearisome human phenomena allotted to every campus for reasons mysterious. One certainly cannot expect a responsible administration to be hopping on circus wagons. Still, it seems so often to be the case —this is an aside—that every year's little knot of agitating students knows at least a partial truth which it is impatient for everybody else to acknowledge. It sees injustice earlier and clearer, and in the case of coeducation as well as curriculum, it sees dead principles institutionalized. ("Doctrinaires are the vultures of principle," said Lloyd George. "They feed upon a principle after it is dead.") Why is it the academic condition that what irritating students have to say must first be brushed off by people old enough and wise enough to know that in the main they are right?

What is a live principle now is that young men and women, by the time they are college age, either are accustomed to regard themselves in complementary relationship to each other, or should be encouraged to adapt quickly to this view. They must be prepared to think and work and eat and sleep with each other upon their own responsibility, master the facility of living in constant interchange, put that behind them and get on with moving through life with ever-expanding breadth. *Now* that is the truth. But I don't think it was our truth, that the perception of ourselves as women had sufficiently unfolded. I don't think, that is, that the idea of retreat for a woman, or retreat for a student *then* needed justification.

Today for Smith to remain a retreat in either the intellectual or sexual sense has to be justified, because the arguments against her staying celibate and remote are very forceful, as it seems to me. What I would want foremost is that she remain academically first class with the broadest reach of sound scholarship possible to an undergraduate college. Given this primacy, other things will or will not fall into place. If I am right about the new girl, for instance, she is early and firmly acclimated to heterosexual life. I hear this as a logical evolution of the species, an enlargement. There are 40 or so men matriculating at Smith this year, larking around this campus in a cheery way, and when I asked a senior (from Dartmouth) why he'd come to Smith, he said he was dumb-founded by the number of people who asked him such a question: by which I inferred that he, male, was early and firmly acclimated to heterosexual life too.

But there is, of course, the other and contrary need in many people (a need I felt then and still feel) to find a haven, privacy; to shy away from coeducational colleges and universities, which seem to harbor madding crowds in a condition of permanent madness. Smith still casts a lovely spell. As I write there even seems to be a pause in revolutionary energy, brought about by surfeit. There is the surfeit of success, since so much change is occurring at Smith, and the surfeit of failure, because the changes are not tailored to the exact specifications of the student master-designers. They're terribly uncompromising, the young.

However amusing it is to have this handful of boys around, it seems essentially a holding operation, and here again, I believe, there is No Time. Already there's the probability, which you may lament or not, that the whole spectrum of temperaments and tastes among qualified girls is not being admitted today as in my day, because the whole spectrum isn't applying. The women's colleges are a little out of joint now because of this, and may become a little more out of joint each year with what has elsewhere become normative. Even if I were not to make a value judgement on this consequence, members of the faculty make it. To keep the widest reach on scholarship you have to hold onto all kinds of them as well as all kinds of bright students.

Those who argue against a precipitous change to coeducation say rightly that, after all, the coeducational universities have been the scenes of the greatest fury and disruption, by comparison with which Smith, Vassar, Amherst, Princeton experience (to date) but a modest seething. It is the kind of argument that can be won on points but that doesn't deal with a massive actuality, somehow. Here are the finest girls still coming to Smith, let's say, still with their eyes open, prepared to venture four years at a women's college. And then, like Joanne, somewhere in the midway they cross over, become almost abruptly new selves, as if they were hatched from fisheries—to go back to the amphibious allusion—and must now have dry ground, the widest horizon, the freest air, with no memory of how nice things were, no gratitude, no patience. There is a surly sullen twist to the discontentment of a women's college campus that distinguishes it from the anger at Harvard or Columbia.

Now, on thinking back upon myself, I assume that I too must have grown through four years, but from what to what? I was a pretty flashy girl, mostly brag, and invited rather extravagant expectations of my performance from faculty and friends, always to have them disconcerted by my ranging from about C-minus to C-plus. About sex I seem to have organized my own uneasy disparate feelings into a political position. I hailed the principled rebel but was shocked by somebody who was reputed to be "promiscuous." Had a girl I knew really entered a Trial Marriage or practiced Free Love, she would have been made a bona fide heroine on my platform, a heroine somewhat vaguely defined, since extra-legal cohabitation does not strike me now as much of a life career. What plans for her waking hours? But she would certainly have been doing a lonely and courageous thing, because the crowd, made of whooshy sentimental reformers of my ilk, might not have rallied to protect her, not knowing then what is known now about protests, demonstrations, demands, confrontations, and *amnesty*. In those days it took guts, but not necessarily, of course, wisdom, now or then, to rebel in this wise.

There were first of all and without question a Father and a Mother standing as stoutly against your personal little sortie into the unconventional as the Pillars of Hercules, with the whole Atlantic oceanful of public opinion behind them. And, on the other side, there was no sea swell of support among the students. Just a few left-wing middle-class girls like me, sympathetic, even charmed by the association, but unreliable, unfinancial, uninformed.

Politically, that is to say, I had bestowed upon all humankind equal sexual rights, whether he be at Princeton or she be at Smith. It was something like extending my personal blessing to their individual relationships, and as useful. In spite of their rights and my blessings it was nearly impossible to have a successful unconventional union because nobody would let you. Your parents wouldn't, the college wouldn't, society wouldn't. Nobody. Where did they get their power?

Power is in the eye of the beholder. I personally can testify that I was landlocked by the power of adulthood.

When I was about Maggie's age, about fifteen, I had a vision of my physical self as being the merest sketch, the barest outlines of the most unadorned human female, still so close in shape and color to the original clay that I was first made of that I was indistinguishable from the mass of lumps walking around—a three-dimensional *tabula rasa,* overweight. Not a good self-image. What I wanted desperately was to dress and adorn and decorate and paint me. The inside of myself was racing, charging, dreaming garish dreams, and I wanted all this to erupt through to the surface, blossom: my skin broke out.

My mother, the arbiter of breeding, her will adumbrated by my father, the Absolute, had me climbing up a ladder of achievements for which the prime rewards that I lusted after would be to wear silk stockings and to use lipstick. The only way I could earn these rewards was to live long enough to be the right age when it was appropriate to the children of our rung—which was very high, we believed—in the Bronx.

It sometimes, but very rarely, crossed my mind that although all my friends wore silk stockings and lipstick before the ages decreed by the eternal rules of breeding, they were not struck dead. They did not obey the rules, and yet life seemed to go on.

I suffered under the rules, sometimes painfully, but I was as cowed by them as if God had made them and was keeping His eye steadily fixed on me, and this may seem particularly odd in a child who was brought up an atheist and never believed in God and never felt any stress about not believing in Him. I was instead entirely intimidated by the household laws, so much so that I rarely had the courage to plead for privileges before their allotted time on the timetable and therefore cheated and lied when overcome by desires, as to wit: I bought pink lip pomade, and after I'd left the house and walked across the park to the subway I'd put it on, very light. And lived in fear that a neighbor would meet my mother and say, "I see Cynthia's wearing lipstick now." That is the sort of thing my guilt and fear were composed of, little sins at enormous expense.

I could not personally entertain the notion of rebelling. It would have been impossible to me even to imagine a dialogue with either of my parents in which I talked back to them, or contradicted them. But sometimes, very rarely, but sometimes, when I witnessed the misbehavior at school of some other child, watched him reprimanded, watched his submission I thought, Suppose he said *No,* and *Just walked Out.* What could they do? What would happen? And with the quickest spin of my mind I saw that the world would come to an end. That is what is happening now, and is it coming to an end? But in those days everybody always obeyed, so far as I knew.

I saw the world would come to an end by an intuitive vision of our whole understanding of life as being a fabrication, all of us being sworn to the truth of this fabrication, and nobody being allowed to defect. Now we are seeing what happens when once they start defecting. I have never ceased to wonder from where my mother drew her absolute power, or, if from the consent of the governed, what made me consent.

By the time I was at College I had been operating for some years as a dual self. My personal behavior was entirely uninfluenced by my political intellection, but on the contrary, altogether determined by the climate of opinion that prevailed on our campus, and that climate kept one cautious, ignorant, immature, and dishonest. It took that first tentative, mischievous impulse of a freshman in the springtime to kick up her heels, as you might say, and discouraged it coldly. By its reinforcement of social and religious and patriotic clichés it retarded your growth through the four years to graduation.

This wasn't Smith, not what the teachers taught, nor what the faculty stood for. This was America at one of the last moments in the history of Western society when its taboos and traditions were still intact. Were I obedient from conviction, were the load of us obedient, from conviction, to all the prescribed rules concerning family, state, church, and the arch-institution, sex, I would have no reason now to look back and say that our maturing was hampered. An unspannable gulf was, however, created by our minds having reached the far shore, exercising the greatest freedom to doubt—indeed, Existentialism was being born then—while our workaday selves followed the streams of expectation that tradition described for women. We could disbelieve, but our imagination under a Hollywood scenarist could not conjure feasible alternatives.

My understanding about the sexual process was probably clinically fairly accurate. You had to take a freshman course called Hygiene 11a, a verging on sex designed in a sort of pincer movement, starting off with toes the first week and proceeding upward to arches, ankles, and knees, and then jumping to the brain and sinuses in about November and moving down. After Christmas there was hung an enormous screen with a large relief map of the uterus in about the eighth week of pregnancy, and we spent the last month on how babies were born. Then we had a semester exam on the safe sinuses, and I didn't pass. What I retained from the course was the impression that that relief map bears an uncanny resemblance to the one of the town of Northampton on the Connecticut River, with the oxbow making a large uterine kink.

While my political position in regard to sexual behavior was liberal and my biological knowledge serviceable in case of need, neither of these aspects had much to do with how I saw myself as a woman, how my generation of women saw themselves, nor how the men saw us.

That a boy and a girl might approach each other with mutual respect—that idea was still on the drawing boards. Among my children and the children I know I see very clearly that mutual respect is the readily offered approach in a new relationship. It is the norm. Though much uncertainty, and also less generous alternatives no doubt lurk at the ready, what a mature student at Smith or Princeton brings to an interchange is an inherent sense of equality—those rights I bestowed, rights that set uneasily on top of one's already finished self, like a crown; those rights were theirs at birth and are deposited in the marrow of their being.

But at Smith in 1948, as well as at Princeton in 1940, the old moral code was only in the process of being discredited. It hadn't let go its hold on your sense of self-respect. Today there is something of a priggishness in the way the avant garde of this generation assumes the right to Make Love. This right supersedes the historical privilege reserved for young males upon the loss of their "innocence," that they were entitled to crow over their coup. The crowing, the possibility that one might be talked about with contempt as an object that was used and discarded, that sordidness still lingered in our minds and clearly in the mind of one Princetonian. As a man you might enjoy a great triumph if you slept with a girl, but you couldn't respect a girl who slept with you. It was a reaching out of the dead hand of the old morality that you couldn't respect her. That was our fear. And with bravado, girls like me used the language somewhat defensively and talked in a businesslike way about Sleeping With someone, but not about Making Love.

So the four years went by and I matured in a manner appropriate to my time, maneuvering through a mating game unconfidently, fearing that my new politics, my finer ethics, were they ventured, would be lost.

VI Unexamined Assumptions

> *"You ought to believe it in perfect faith, since the Sorbonnists say that faith lies in believing things that possess no appearance of likelihood."*
>
> Gargantua

Life: this fabrication to which we swore fealty fitted together like the interlocking of a thousand-piece jigsaw puzzle, and every piece was an unexamined assumption. A real puzzle buff doesn't succumb to the angry suspicion that the manufacturer has carelessly mixed two of his products—an amateur may, but not a real puzzle buff. Buffs of anything are the smilers in the world: they have confidence that in the end everything fits together.

I loved to do jigsaw puzzles, and even after several of the children were born I'd finish one up (at night, by the sea, in a rented cottage in terrible light) with the sense of a real job done, like all the ironing, or all the hems. I would look at it and see that it was beautiful. But no more. Because I've been lured, throughout this past decade, to pick up first one and then another neat if knobby unexamined assumption and examine it. Jenny and Nora have the border of "The Drummer Boy" (in Civil War grey) set up on a bridge table in the television room, and they want me please to come and do it with them for a little while. I do. But in five minutes—and to my nervous surprise, which is why I record this—I push away from the table and say sharply, "I can't. I hate doing puzzles." Ex-buff.

At no one point slipped out of me the need to have everything fit, be resolved. I never consciously relinquished a preference for a first-class ideology, and for trust in a happy ending. Life was a puzzle, yes, perhaps; but all the pieces were on the board and could be perfectly inserted if you had a good eye for it. And I had a good eye for puzzles—that that was my view is no wonder. Over my immutable world presided Franklin D. Roosevelt, coming into office when I was six, which I do not remember, and remaining steadfast at the helm until I was nineteen, a freshman at Smith and mature enough to take the personal loss, as personal loss it was for citizens of Bronx County. And fleshing out the meaning of the Manichaean world of Roosevelt—the New Deal and the invincible forces for good on the one side, and Hitler coming up on the other—was the movies. It has yet to be calculated what influence Heyday Hollywood had in shaping the responses, political, psychological, moral of my America, its captive audience.

But as to one nation indivisible, can Tony and our girls have anything like my experience of Presidential wrong-righting rule, these children who have known days of funeral-watching on the telly, who are connoisseurs of detail in regard to riderless horse and empty boot: funerals of an assassinated president, an assassinated president-to-be (for whom I would have voted), an old president, and non-presidents. I know that the sense of real immutability comes from the father and mother whose certitude in my case was underwritten by the undefeatable President Roosevelt, a reinforcement reserved for Democratic families, perhaps. Pit that against our children's world in which noble Jack Kennedy is cut down just before (*just before,* as his friends say) his great surge towards his prime, and *that* followed by the astonishing success of pedestrian men, a decade's documentary of ignoble *American* deeds; and it is pitting immutability against mutability plain.

The fabrication of unexamined assumptions which was my reality had as its prime property this immutability, not because there was no such thing as historical change. Clearly there had been incredible change through history. But now we were in Modern Times, very well named too, a kind of final stage that was to stretch out (a bit dully, I feared) into the infinite future. It may be difficult to look back upon the depression, the New Deal, and World War II as a pretty flat scene, but it was not difficult living through it to find it flattish.

I was given to reflecting sadly but not long, when I was about twelve, that the events in the world surrounding me were mundane beyond retrieving and could therefore never conceivably become History, (say Cleopatra and you see bangs, say Pilgrims, Dolly Madison, Queen Elizabeth, and their historical skirts reach down'to the floor), take on the flavor and hue of an era. The very style of the clothes I wore was not a style at all but a final, logically-arrived-at, never-to-be-changed right thing for girls to wear. Saddle shoes and socks and pleated skirts just covering the knee and blouses and cardigan sweaters, and how adeptly I rolled my hair with two fingers into an unbecoming artificial pompadour held in place by such a mass of deep-dug bobby pins so that my scalp felt as though it was clamped on by metal strips. All that is left of this conviction is that blouses and pleated skirts and cardigans are the right thing for an adolescent to wear. Each fall I bring them out, lovely pleated wool skirts in several sizes for all the girls, and Maggie or Jenny will smile encouragingly and receive their lot politely and hang them up nicely and never wear them.

As I believed that what I wore was the inevitable culmination of human striving to discover what people *ought* to wear, so did I know that all knowledge was known, and that what remained to be done was to apply it to get rid of the evils left over from history. History per se preceded Modern Times and did not advance much beyond the Civil War, played by Mr. President Lincoln looking exactly like Raymond Massey, as I among several million people can testify. And who is Raymond Massey, Mother? Raymond Massey, child, was President Lincoln, and I'm not going to go into it. I didn't know then that we were living at the tail-end of an epoch that began with the Italian Renaissance and tight-thinking unsentimental spiritual fathers like Machiavelli, and that Edward G. Robinson, Humphrey Bogart, John Wayne, Errol Flynn at the Radio City Music Hall were to represent its final arty flourish. And I certainly believed that the Radio City Music Hall was the first example of the final statement of what all architecture was intended to become: Modern.

Everything fitted in that rational, logical, progressive, knowing, severely unmysterious world. There were no conundrums. Puzzles, but nothing metaphysical. Each question was susceptible of an answer. Today there are no answers, and if I grew up through those eventful years finding them flattish, and now in this apocalyptic age am liable to bouts of exultation, it is not so much in spite of my thinking that history is indeed continuing, right to its end, but because of the excitement, through reading, of watching how. I'm ex-buff, but not ex-smiler. Out of my box, as against Pandora's, I let fly away all the absolutes save that one, which is to read and save me.

I get up early in the morning and I read so as to be toe-to-toe with what's up and what's coming up, more or less in the spirit in which Christopher Robin was careful to watch his feet, not step on the lines but keep in the squares, to prevent himself from being eaten by bears.

Now in particular it has been through essays and reviews and occasionally the book itself that I have learned how historians and biographers have converted whole hunks of the recent past—that hundred years of blank which, were I called upon to identify in my schooldays I would have divided in two and misnamed Victorian, (1860–1914), and Modern, (1914–Forever)—that hundred years being the rich source of my great body of unexamined assumptions, and not only mine.

Watch them, these new historians, as they rend the veils of seemliness, of successful self-discipline and piety, of orderly family life and love and sexual regularity, from the hard-core humans who lived in England and America and Western Europe through my blank. They seem to be able to palpate real veins through the thin skin of this past, and surmise the most widespread personal human frailty of the most recognizably modern complexity. I draw comfort not from evidence of the fallen state of our Christian ancestors, but through concluding that we haven't fallen so precipitously after all, from something higher and healthier and *realer* and *righter*. And it is a comfort non-readers in the Now Generation are not likely to come upon; and more than that, more than a comfort missed, is a perspective wanting.

Not that I would deny we are in a parlous condition. Never more parlous. But this is only because technology has put into our hands the tools to finish us off in any of several ways. Our ancestors, even less prone than we to self-doubt, less insightful, less informed, had they our tools, probably would not have let man skid through by the skin of his teeth, as I am hoping we will do, not climb the forty-fourth rung. And here I draw upon an interview in *The Manchester Guardian* with Herman Kahn, a chilly man from a think tank, "the theoretician of unthinkable war," who devised the "escalation ladder," the forty-four thermonuclear strategic rungs which begin with "subcrises maneouvering" and end with "spasm of insensate war, when Mr. President or his opposite numbers go off their heads and press the button as a reflex."

This is a given, now, the ending of all life, our supremest know-how. So it would seem not a bit too early for historiography to widen and deepen its concern with understanding the past by tentative exploration of the senses, the passions, the emotional portraits of kings and women and thinkers and their constituencies, the populations that allowed them their power. And there are coming to light private personal patterns that had remained tastefully unrecorded, buried under the patina of appropriate and proper public behavior. These patterns deal with the play of the senses, the sensitive, the insensate; trivial or sordid or sensational as they might appear, they did in their way and in their time play with the events that made our past and hence our present.

In the last few years, for instance, there has been a peering into the Edwardian era, into the years before World War I and into the lives of the young men who were to be among the great seminal thinkers of our Modern century—men like Bertrand Russell, John Maynard Keynes, G. E. Moore. From their diaries and autobiographical notes one may catch the tastes, the tone, the style of intellectual society, through the war which decimated it and beyond into Bloomsbury and the interbellum period, actually that very same flat era of my growing up that seems astonishingly historical to me now. Well, historians are intruding upon the privacy of this recent past, revealing strange and persistent sexual vagaries and patterns of pathology in our Western social scheme. In England the uncovering of the extensive and widely practiced Oxbridge "fad" of homosexuality had been unsettling but instructive. I remember reading an essay in which it was suggested that since the Foreign Office was virtually staffed by graduates of Oxford and Cambridge in the decades between the wars, this overwhelming sexual ambivalence, where it wasn't firm homosexuality, and this Bloomsbury mystique must have marked significantly the government's responses to events from 1920 to 1939.

I feel there's a parallel in the marking of my generation,

which grew up having life described and interpreted for it by
Hollywood. Like Oxbridge homosexuality, Hollywood's influence in America on all classes, one way or another, through
those years of my formation was incisive and for life. More
bludgeon than pestle, it ground into the mortar of us moral-
istic attitudes and mechanical responses which reinforce the
rigid and ungenerous qualities in our American nature to
this day, and for a long time to come. A national problem,
the killed imagination. That we don't readily see ourselves
and the fatuousness and embarrassment of our moralizing
as we might otherwise have been able to do is due to this
conditioning through childhood by Hollywood. How many
sunny Saturday afternoons did I sit in a darkened movie
house under a navy blue sky where stars twinkled and pale
clouds sailed, and then come out blinking and dizzy, with
my sense of time in disorder for a while and my sense of
values in disorder indefinitely? Hundreds. Hundreds of sunny
Saturday afternoons I sat in the dark and rejoiced in the
denial of human complexity, a denial that was pummeled flat
down into the senses, permanently disqualifying a terrible lot
of us from ever really sorting things out.

Hollywood captured banality and never let it go. It did
not, of course, design our fabrication of reality but—to
return to the analogy of the jigsaw puzzle—it was by all odds
the greatest manufacturer of the product and, with its single
press, cut *ad infinitum* the same interlocking pieces of card-
board, upon which had been glued thousands of Drummer
Boys or thousands of Grand Canals of Venice, or thousands
of Autumn Scenes. Every piece fit, and Age of Buffs that
it was, there was no inclination to jam a piece where it didn't

belong. Then nothing would have fit. On some level of our consciousness, I believe, we saw that.

My children are television babies whose impression of any program should it be the least bit positive is always corrected by one parent or the other, neither of whom ever watches but superintends their reception by providing a wholesome aura of contempt. This is very good for the children as it turns out, for it has made them sharp and critical, and in an argument between the generations over whether it is *ever* worthwhile, we have been licked several times. Their approach to the movies is even more selective, their tastes running to French and Swedish films. They are as knowledgeable by fifteen and sixteen about the wildly permeating qualities of violence and sex in our society as I was at about thirty-seven. What I thought about violence at their ages was Nothing. It hadn't been recognized to be the oldest American trait. It hadn't been recognized at all.

About sex. I try to fix my mind on what I could have thought at fourteen, but this mind seems always to dart off towards some adolescent action as though it were not able to locate any interior whatsoever inside that actress, the child star, me. Were I able to contract myself backwards I see that I would be unidentifiable were I not viewed through the film of artificial superfiber spun by Hollywood scriptwriters: and to this very moment I can hardly believe, and find it surely inexcuseable, that I should have been caught for life by the simple-minded cliché-riddled formulas that the movies presented as the Entire Picture, as the whole human repertoire. So that by the time I was in college, in spite of my intellectual liberation in the matter of sex, and in spite of my bestowing

on women all rights and privileges (but, I believe, not responsibilities) pertaining thereto, and altogether regardless of
my personal blessing upon any sort of liaison (of integrity)
however unconventional, my own imagination had only the
limited and appallingly banal materials irradiated upon it in
a blackened orchestra through a girlhood of Saturday mat-
inees, and very nearly *only* these materials with which to
project a future for myself. A kind of radiation sickness
might be expected to be the consequence. I eschewed the
wavy knee-dips of Betty Grable and strove upwards towards
Ingrid Bergman: a class orientation.

Nothing could be more modern than the movies, nothing
more immutable than the life it depicted. The very movement
of the moving picture was illusory. It did not move. It went
nowhere, and I went nowhere with it. It was a stasis, a kind
of still frame in which conventional morality was immobilized,
glamorized, reinforced. There was no way out, not even—
this being a visual medium—through the mind's eye. So that
read Good Books though I did, and aspire to the intellectual
position (?) of Ingrid Bergman as I might, and more than
that, be as superior as she to the behavioral requirements of
ordinary people, I was anyhow hopelessly obedient to the
lessons of Hollywood's University of Life, as I was to the
requirements of my biology.

In the *Times* the other day I read a brief interview with a
remarkable man named Birdwhistell who said, among other
things, "I think it's foolish for one man and one woman to get
married and to set themselves the task of supplying all the
other's emotional needs. . . ." It is the exact opposite of the
Hollywood Doctrine of Morality. The exact opposite. A movie

could no more have implied this than it could have shown a man and woman naked in bed, sheets albeit up to the chin. But today's young suspect that it is true, that it is unreasonable for man or woman to place the entire burden of providing meaning and contentment upon one's marriage partner, and meanwhile the movies they've been seeing since the eighth grade have presented material for their imagination which on the one hand is very often undeniably gross, but on the other rather nobly affirms woman's sexual equality—that she is equal in vulnerability, equal in desire—and woman's self-respect, and I think provide their fantasy of love and passion with the addition of dignity.

It was my own curious limitation (perhaps my own) that while I could acknowledge the sexual act as a physical performance, it was out of the range of possibility to think of a woman lying naked by a man, looking into his face, seeing even so much as a bare neck and bare shoulders. Or just the eyes—to look into his eyes would be an unbearable exposure more of soul than body. What could have accounted for her being in such a position while still retaining her self-respect? Nothing Hollywood uncovered.

Hollywood was the underwriter for all unexamined assumptions.

VII   Anythingarian

. . . the gaping contrast between the richness of life and the poverty of all possible formulas.

WILLIAM JAMES

As a resident of Smith one would be, of course, in the neighborhood of twenty years old. A block beyond the college, an assortment of Victorian houses is strung out—I loosely name them Victorian to suggest American turn-of-the-century variety and middle size. We live there, and by the most morale-boosting chance, we live in bibulous good fellowship with householders in the neighborhood of forty years old. Not all are of this advanced age, but we are preponderant, and it's our weight you feel on the east end of Harrison Avenue, by God.

When the weather warms and the days lengthen, we come out of the woodwork into the evenings and onto the porch stoops, and ignore yardsful of children. We talk, and retain the most delicate respect for each other's privacy and sometimes mind each other's business terribly. There is a kind of cabal, and our own householder, who is self-certified as most artistic and as having the best taste, acts as color chairman when anybody else's house needs painting and is being constantly harassed by indications that his opinion will be ignored. A philosopher across the street, employed by the college, and *not* a drifter regardless of appearances and the fact he came from Canada, went ahead anyway and trimmed his house in yellow. Saskatoon baroque, Paul calls it.

About half the men are faculty. The man most loved, his opinions most respected, is not at Smith, and in fact not an intellectual at all, and his wife tends not to give a damn what color our Paul thinks her house should be painted. She is necessary ballast.

On a Thursday near supper time the sky turned suddenly dark, and a hurricane of a wind hurled itself into the valley, and large whorls of it ragged the great trees on our block fiercely, as if frantic dogs had had them between their teeth. Well, it brought everybody out, ladies as well, the full complement. We're a fearless lot, and we stood under the trees, any one of which might have fallen, for all we knew. Then across from us there was a tremendous crack. It was an elm about to split, an elm that is so tall you never notice that the top branches alone would make a row of six or eight good-sized trees. There was the crack, and the branches continued to wave wildly, but nothing came down. We ambled—this is a cool group—to a safe point of observation. I observed to myself that it wasn't safe and, I observed out loud that I saw a tree fall like that in a movie and kill a girl.

All remained unalarmed, untouched by my warning. A tree-sized branch fell and crushed the hood of an empty car. The effect was fine and was admired quietly.

"But she was a lesbian," I added, ashamed of my having expressed alarm, and Hollywood-reared as I was, acknowledging that because none of us was a lesbian there had been no real cause for anxiety.

And they, in their 40s, my age group, were Hollywood-reared too, and so whether or not they saw this particular motion picture, understood that trees fell on lesbians but not on mothers, of which all these women were samples—not even on the mother of the graduate. We were Hollywood's children whose responses were programmed, to use the word retroactively, through the infant stages of the communications revolution. In each of us had been installed a beautifully crystallizing, narrowing, tidying, limiting reflex, that conditioned us to observe in a singular way: to observe in order to pare, denature, and extract a moral lesson, a patriotic moral lesson. A tree would not fall on an American mother. Flip a pebble into the surface of *our* pool and the ripples contract, grow smaller and smaller.

I'm taken with the picture of the ripples growing smaller, but actually, conditioned though we certainly were to snatch up every living thing that impressed our minds and rinse it of its own colors and shadings and trim it to fit into the formal framework of our known world, that known world is simply gone, has dropped precipitously down and backwards into history after all, and seems at its least destructive, unbelievably naive and quaint. There were no lesbians in the movies of that known world. Lots of mothers but absolutely no lesbians.

There were no lesbians, no ironies, no naked bodies alive or dead, no irreconcilable conflicts, no creditable exploration of social ills, but I have to say this in a plaintive aside, there was *no boredom*. Boredom, like sex and violence, simply hadn't been recognized either as American or as Art. *Now* I have been taught by this Cultural Medium, the Cinema, that it is both, and though I'm no critic, I agree they do it marvelously and I am. My reactions to all the movies I saw in my childhood, as I recollect them, ranged from good to wonderful, and they were as likely to make me yawn as make me think. *C'est ça.* Still, the proposition that in boredom our society has democratized, so to speak, an affliction once confined to a small leisure class is an interesting idea that needed statement.

We graze along the edge of the sidewalk, this lowing herd of parents, and watch the branch fall across the car hood, and we keep our cool; just as we follow the Smith girls in their bitterness, a bitterness unseemly and untimely, and watch their efforts to dismantle the college community, and we keep our cool: and beyond that we monitor the violence on the left and the right tearing up the country, and we keep our cool. This cool is, of course, cover first of all for despair, but not despair over the loss of that known world. Each of us without doubt finds his own place in the spectrum of responses to each event in the revolutions, but none of us, as I hazard to speak this single time for our neighborly herd, none is more than marginally rueful about the functional excellence of the past, of that immutable world of absolutes that made us. The rue is for the loss of subtle, lovely, civilized kindnesses now deemed expendable.

The cool is, second of all and in *me,* cover for a deep joy in being freed of defending or living with the disparity I have talked about between one's lofty ethical aspirations for humankind, and the most compromising inaction: I have been freed, by these assorted youth-led revolutions, from living with or defending that particular American Way of

Life. This is also the consequence of an evolution in my self-awareness of which this book is a chart—unintended, but after all a chart.

My self-awareness grew in interactions with a world wired by a popular culture just at the very beginning of its being up to electronic tricks—still formal, rational, hysterically simplistic—while my children are born into that world detonated, born into an exploding galaxy of uncensored information, unmoralized experience, unorganized factual knowledge. They are born into a society in which the electronic triumphs are no longer being fed with cultural absolutes that reinforce political conformity, religious conservatism, the way it was in the beginning for us, with radio and the movies, at that early innocent stage of any device, where you feed it what's available to watch it work for the joy of watching it work. Just as it happened when I brought home a food blender, after twenty years of marriage, so that I could make curried mayonnaise the way my friend Brett does. All the children want to make it work, and we'll stick anything into it, try anything, rifle through the cupboards to see what we have in the way of ingredients, and are enchanted by confecting banana milkshakes although not by eating them. (So far I hate the blender.)

The first insight that my world was fabricated, animated, and controlled by wires came to me so late—not, in fact, until my senior year in college—that I marvel all these years later at my tardiness. It can be accounted for by two factors: I was disabled by coming to Smith from a Democratic New Deal background. I was disarmed by having no religion. All my friends, and what I estimate to be a laudable majority of my peers spent their first years moving politically from right to left and the rest of their time consolidating. As concerns personal travail, they had the soul's wrangle with the God of their fathers. I had nothing fundamental to reorder (I thought) but remained more or less exercised by a running appraisal of current events, and a not very discerning appraisal at that, certainly not an *informed* appraisal. If I don't see in many of today's young the girl I was, I recognize that category of outrage at social injustice that can be maintained at fever pitch without the fuel of facts.

As to God, I was taught at an early age that there were three ancient deities at the source of our culture, Zeus, Jehovah and Jesus, and there things were left for a long while. When I picked up their stories again it was with some surprise that I learned they had not retained equal status. Never was I taught to pray, neither was I taught to mock, and rarely have I felt either inclination.

In the semester before my graduation I took a seminar in which we were to read *The New York Times* and the New York *Herald Tribune* every day and be responsible for describing the difference in the reporting of each news item. The *Herald Tribune* was at its last fine moment before its decline, and the *Times* had not come into its great days which are now: be aware of great days while you are living through them, if you can. What we were to learn was that there is no such thing as objective reporting, no such thing as straight news. Everything printed has been processed by the human mind. We learned this.

Looking back it seems not only a bit late, but more than a bit obvious, and there's the fact that our Jenny who is in the sixth grade has got the message already.

"Do you want to know the reason I like to study Argentina?" she asked me at breakfast this morning. "It is because the people in that country have an orderly life and are happy."

"Why Jenny," said the mother, startled and once more annoyed by evidence that the Northampton Public School system operates out of textbooks written in the dismal years of the 50s when our side were all happy freedom-lovers and their side were very sneaky. "The front page of the *Times* has been running an account of Argentine riots all week."

"I knew it! Every time I think I might have found a country with happy people in it, it turns out to be a very babyish story written by a really wrong historian."

Imagine, at the age of eleven, making room for the fallibility of the printed word, and behind that word a fallible man.

And Julie's eleventh-grade class in American History spent an hour last year gleefully picking out howlers in their text by comparing a 1956 edition with a sample of the new revised edition thoughtfully sent on by the publisher. ("Many domestic slaves were kindly cared for by their masters and led very happy lives." to "Robbed of their human dignity, no slave could be said to lead a satisfactory life.")

Imagine, at sixteen, reading with a sophistication that not only measures the history and the historian, but spots the publisher's ploy.

I was a full grown woman, finishing Smith, having had nothing fundamental inside me to reorder in the way of a political and religious identity, but was nonetheless, as it is clear to me now, as undoubting a believer in that world as Cotton Mather was in his.

About this first tentative modest but fateful (for me) step I didn't even know I took outside the Compleat Moderne Worlde: it was just a paw through the door, the paw of a political animal in a political world. What happened in the course of the years following that seminar is that I became accustomed to account for a human agency as interpreter of that Compleat Moderne Worlde, a retailer, a relayer who organized his impression of the events he was hired to record according to his political and ethical bias. The best of his breed would strive to compensate for the bias, the worst to manipulate his audience, and there were a lot of worsts. Ineradicable personal bias, I discovered, was one sorry human failing I had overlooked, but one that certainly made more complicated the romp along the road to progress.

I was still working with the same pieces inside the same framework, only they were now sticky. Human bias, once ascertained, was what you spent your life rising above, although you couldn't. I will go to my grave, no doubt, harried by the impossible demands of that Old Testament God whether I will or not believe in him, who drove half my ancestors across the ocean from Bohemia, so as they could pair up with the other half, who had the longer trek of a couple of centuries up through France to Amsterdam. Saints, these latter were, and what in part I stem from, poor, weak, back-sliding saints given to hysteria.

Before the seminar—the world the stage, I a player—life's rule was to perform as gloriously as possible (like Mrs. Miniver—wife and mother; like Shaw's St. Joan—for principle; like Rosalind Russell—for Cary Grant) the various roles assigned by Necessity, and any balky little disinclination inside me that raised its head got bopped with the dull end of the cleaver. The seminar introduced relativism into my rigid mind, but gently, in a non-threatening way. I had become immobilized by a simple belief in progress and the precise behavior, manifestly, it demanded of me. It was a kind of absolute that I was stuck at, and I felt the strain. With this little jarring by the seminar, this introduction of a Counter-Necessity—to make allowance for the human agency, for human fallibility (and from there off and away to human *variability*), I started rolling slowly towards the Anythingarian end of thought (Joyce's word) like the ribbon of my type-writer when it has reached the end of one spool and strains and is finally released to unwind the other spool all the way. Well, I'm not going all the way.

But Anythingarianism is a name to put in lights on top of today's Scene. My children are at home in this Scene, are formed by this Culture, and I find I must depart from Matthew Arnold's meaning and acknowledge the extension, *now,* of culture spread wider than reading, observing, thinking, although I can't adapt to it, my nervous system is not tuned to it, wired for it, plugged in. The din is terrible to me. Their music is an incessant, pervasive, agitated racket, and I do what I can not to hear it. I never have watched television, while they never haven't, so I can only sob over the influence, but I don't know what it is.

But I see the movies they see (and am always surprised there is no formula, no happy ending, that nothing fits, that a film has left me on my own). I watch the acting out of human passions unimaginable to me in my girlhood, indeed startling to me still, and Maggie, not sixteen, watches too. It will hardly come as a shock to her that making love tends to be a naked business. Yes, she certainly knows what lesbians are and is compassionate, but she doesn't think they invariably meet their deaths by having trees fall on them. It is in fact characteristic of Maggie to allow for a human agency, for human fallibility, for human variability, and this seems to be true of most of the young I know.

Maggie, Jenny, and I together watched a fourteen-year-old Juliet, altogether credibly a child still, with the sweet round unfinished face of a child and the sweet round nearly finished body of a woman, burst with love and passion. When I was their ages I would have found it unthinkable for a girl of fourteen to experience what was reserved in my mind for eighteen. Privileges accumulated with time and life was a kind of progress from Nothing—in the neighborhood of which I felt I was—to Everything, my destination. I allowed that at eighteen you could fall passionately in love. But my children, in a firm and respectful way, insist that each person is ready for this or that thing in his life at his own time, and they are very unwilling to set a lower limit on the ages of readiness— not for making a political judgment, not for making love. They don't believe they are in the neighborhood of nothing, and I don't believe they are.

VIII On Violation

That element of tragedy which lies in the very fact of frequency, has not yet wrought itself into the coarse emotion of mankind; and perhaps our frames could hardly bear much of it. If we had a keen vision and feeling of all ordinary human life, it would be like hearing the grass grow and the squirrel's heart beat, and we should die of that roar which lies on the other side of silence.

GEORGE ELIOT

Here is somebody like me born into a world where all the pieces fit, and that world is now shattered; it and all its parts, fragmented, every moment breaking more apart. But I slipped into an interlude of disarming calm when I walked down Elm Street this last Memorial Day to watch the parade, weaving first among all our townspeople preparing themselves on the lawns of the college. The brassiest were the bands, the high school band in the navy-blue uniform of the Park Avenue doorman, braided gold aiguillette looping down from one shoulder, the junior high school band suffering the restraint merely of red blazers, being tried and, only if proven, elevated to doorman with busby—I forgot the busbys—doormen at Buckingham Palace; the Legionnaires, the Girl Scouts, the Boy Scouts, the Ladies Auxiliaries—and no battalions from any of the three revolutions in that parade, no. The sun on this New England morning is so bright it is almost a sound, and the children and I have come to cheer Maggie marching with her bass clarinet in red jacket. The sense of consolidating, benign communal good will is nearly dizzying as I walk with the neighbor I love and we stop and talk to other people I like and love and we stop and go, stop and go on. Is it still role-playing? Am I now materfamilias, the conservator?

And here are my children, born into that world bursting like the Fourth of July—a memory of bursting they haven't even got (but I have it and for old joy it is second only to Christmas)—coolly putting one foot before the other to the rhythm of *Seventy-Six Trombones*. Not to *The Green Berets*. For as to the three revolutions, they have their farm teams in the schools of our town, but there are other schools in this agricultural valley who lend their bands to our parade, bands much better than ours, snappy, trim, who clip along smartly as bands are supposed to do. *The Green Berets* is in their repertoire.

We are a middle-class nation, remember, and in that guise we were assembled for that one hour that one May morning. When I was growing up, I heard about a poll that asked All Americans what class they believed they belonged to, and ninety-five percent said the Middle Class. I found this such a gratifyingly dear and democratic testimony to the success of the American Experiment, patriotic child that I was. We were a classless society practically, it seemed to prove. That is the kind of information poll-takers are delivered of: mouses. Patriotic woman that I now am, I must identify an American mouse and squeal when I see one.

Well, there they are, our children, warming up in the farm teams and yet still able to set a busby on top of a face adorned with mustache and earlocks—Buckingham Palace recruiting its doormen from the yeshiva—and I thought of them when I read about the mummers in *The Return of the Native,* youths who took part annually in the Christmas pageants, this in about 1840 in rural England.

"For the mummers and mumming Eustacia had the greatest contempt. The mummers themselves were not afflicted with any such feeling for their art, though at the same time they were not enthusiastic. A traditional pastime is to be distinguished from a mere revival in no more striking feature than in this, that while in the revival all is excitement and fervour, the survival is carried on with a stolidity and absence of stir which sets one wondering why a thing that is done so perfunctorily should be kept up at all. Like Balaam and other unwilling prophets, the agents seem moved by an inner compulsion to say and do their allotted parts whether they will or no. This unweeting manner of performance is the true ring by which, in this refurbishing age, a fossilized survival may be known from a spurious reproduction."

"Unweeting," beautiful word, is "unwitting, *Archaic,*" and an unweeting manner of performance tells in a million little things I do, and have passed on and my children do, the great body of my composite self either remaining unexamined or having been examined cursorily and retained perfunctorily. But my children have a much finer eye, or perhaps it would be better to say much sterner eye, for fossilized survival, *because* their known world is the bursting one, and I believe that, should they in their time walk down Elm Street in the summer sunshine, it will be a one hundred percent spurious reproduction that they watch, and I worry whether they will be warmed by love for their neighbors.

You wonder as you look from this dear old parade to the frightening new chaos, about students at an age whose needs for orderly meaning, for moral beauty, for ideology and its blood-bonds of fellowship—so intense, these needs, as to seem physiological—you wonder why they are incessant and insatiable in furthering the disruption of this already most acutely disordered planet. Brash, callow, insensitive, unsubtle zealots, they can't even love a parade. I love a parade. I stand on Elm Street under an elm and marvel at this picture of peace and prosperity, of children marching in the band, Old Glory fluttering—several Old Glories in fact—fluttering for old wars and an old revolution: not for our carnage, our new revolutions, our violence now, and I see that we are standing in a still frame from an old movie, standing at the edge of the college lawns, the college at our backs.

Our backs to the college, people of my age, our side, hear the outraged students protest, and we exclaim, out of a reasonable irritation that is a respectable part of our ethical code, that the young are only negative, that they are prescribing nothing positive, that they are only demanding and disdain to propose, "that the first step is to bring down with a crash the whole existing structure, the second it was premature to discuss," is them in a nutshell. Bring it all down, this pretty town, this lovely elm-umbrellaed street, our children, our fluttering flags, this finest woman's college in the world, this finest, oldest, best.

But absolutely, our exclamation cuts no ice with the girls

on the campus, the finest, youngest, best.

Because when we look back over our shoulders to the campus we see only disruption and disintegration. We don't catch on. We miss, first of all, the near literalness with which they honor the Judeo-Christian ethic, and we don't see, second, the tremendous underlying *order* that gives form to what looks to us like a shattered world. This is an order that imposes a unitary, consolidating, interlocking network of causes for their finding intolerable what they find intolerable, and they find intolerable every fact of life that comes to their attention. This underlying order produces the unitary, consolidating, interlocking network of intolerable consequences. And I see it their way. *Now* I see it their way, that our demand that they respect family, church, country, and even the oldest women's college in the world are mad demands. *Their* demands are so bad-mannered—but we make allowances for the vocabulary of the revolution, and in our largess we recognize an attention-getting device and in our wisdom we don't overreact—our side, the best on our side are careful not to overreact. Their demands are so provocative. Our demands are mad.

I will just let today's *Times* bear witness to this, to how, reading it from their side, all the pieces interlock that make us ponderous, good-hearted, virtue-loving, concerned—concern is a noted feature of my own face ("there will be time to prepare a face to meet the faces that you meet . . .")—evil-doers. But I must say first that I draw my own insight from Hannah Arendt's phrase, "the banality of evil," the subtitle of her book on Eichmann, and in that phrase I find implicit the indictment for complicity of so many fine people in the success of things like the Final Solution.

For our complicity, looking at the *Times,* I ignore Vietnam, where it is too obvious that we are brutalizing ourselves; and the Military-Industrial-Labor complex, where it is too obvious that in a banal, responsible way millions of people, good clerks to good generals, are employed in a bureaucracy of brutalization: and the testimony of Welfare mothers about the indignities of the Free Lunch program, humane voices remarkable for their coming out of what ought to have been a totally brutalized proletariat. I ignore what is to me obvious, and lift another rock: a large other rock from God's country now rock-strewn.

Just a day's piece of news this is. There has been a special inquiry into a corner of the New York judiciary system, stemming from a case of four Long Island Railroad passengers who were jailed overnight for refusing, as a protest against overcrowding and lack of heat on their train, to show their tickets to a conductor. The condition of trains tracking back and forth along the Eastern Corridor—that's where I live transportwise, the Easterncorridor—is unbelievably sordid. What we who use them have to struggle with is the unbelief. But here again I spare a little nostalgic ache that my children will not have to spare, for lovely train rides in gracious trains, and for the memory of waiting with mounting excitement on summer Friday evenings at the Center Moriches station for the train that would bring my father with Schraffts ice cream packed in dry ice from the city for his weekend with us. And that train, with its white-coated attendants, was a quite elegant Long Island Railroad train, in the not-really-so-distant past. My world had lovely trains, and I sigh for them. For what can our young grow nostalgic in the public transportation line? An abrasive experience with public transportation is the only experience the young know. That we have tolerated this "decline" in public amenities—and they don't even know how long we have tolerated this decline, which is at least to the extent of my whole adult life—is merely one piece in their interlocking consequence-puzzle—but not the piece I want to push into place here.

Here were these four indignant passengers, three women and a man in their twenties, pitched to a protest—they would *not* present their tickets—pitched then into an experience with the law, which, the inquiry said, had a "Kafkaesque quality." Brought before a judge with a "brusque and arbitrary attitude, an absence of concern," they seemed to have been processed through several houses of correction or whatever they are, because of overlapping administrative authority. "The conduct of the arraignment of those passengers was inexcusable, and the procedures employed in the Women's House of Detention following their arraignment were humiliating and offensive to human dignity"—and bring to the fore the issue of whether "rectal and vaginal searches" are necessary to satisfy some question that would otherwise remain unanswered about railroad passengers who don't show their tickets.

I cannot bear this Kafkaesque quality. I could bear, just barely bear, the Dickensian quality of human misery that came to my attention in my childhood, the starved and the exploited in a political world. But we have become too psychologically aware now. Has the machinery of government become this, a kind of relentless, mindless invasion of the sanctity of human dignity, the violation of the body *and* the soul? Does it administer the routine smearing of human sensibilities by a regular impersonal bureaucratic procedure? Is it no more than a vast interlocking *apparat* inviolate—but the people are violated and at the end are dismissed with cards that say DO NOT BEND, DO NOT MUTILATE. That kind of Kafkaesque quality, were we to let ourselves encompass the fact of its frequency, would surely have us "die of that roar which lies on the other side of silence."

Let me proceed more slowly through this harrowing eastern-corridor of a world where cards are not bent or mutilated, but human beings are; let me retrace my steps of shock, if I can, from that woman who loves a parade, who felt a patriot's joy standing there on the college lawn, in the still frame of a technicolor movie, green and yellow with trees and sunshine, red, white and blue with our flags, *primary colors;* to the woman who hovers uneasy and nonviolent by the barricades. Adamant at the barricades are dirty, self-righteous, arrogant, naive, DEMANDING students who condemn us out of hand because we are immoral, we and all our institutions, family, church, country, college, and they will not trade their human birthright for this monstrous mess of pottage. Fastidious, I keep off to the side, offended by their dirty, self-righteous, arrogant, naive, and demanding ways, and believe we are immoral.

Actually I was not near the barricades at all but on the porch, rocking in the rocking chair with today's *Times* clutched against my stomach, my heart blanched by this story of the four railroad passengers, because first of all I can easily see Julie or Maggie, with their sense of responsible

citizenship already acutely developed, accept the invitation
to protest against terrible conditions in a railroad car. A most
peaceful, decorous protest it would seem to be to me who still
detests violence, and, above all, violence engendered by our
side. And then I could see myself accept this invitation. And
then I could see that I was dividing people up between those
who are suitable to be the sisters, wives, mothers of, for
instance, Princeton men, and for whom it is inconceivable
that they should be drawn downwards into that black eastern-
corridor, and other people, God knows who they are, but
doubtless legions and legions of them who spend a lot of time
in and out of that corridor—a corridor through which people
are filing all the time, year in and year out, legions of them
that rarely come to the attention of one's conscience.

I then consider this underworld in New York City, beyond
which, vaguely defined, are other underworlds in how many
other American cities. But I do not consider it a criminal
underworld. For old times' sake one must cling to the concept
that people are innocent until proven guilty, all these legions
of people, innocent, who are brought to the precinct station,
brought next before city court judges, brought then to the
houses of correction. Well, it must require an enormous
bureaucratic arrangement, with judges and clerks and police
and jailers and matrons—*apparat* inviolate, manned (and
womaned) by people who themselves must be regarded as
innocent until proven brutalized by the jobs they do (if not
brutalized earlier). And even whether or not you consider
that all these people are innocent or all guilty, the violation is
intolerable.

After imagining the shock to the sensibilities of my girls

and me consequent upon not having a railroad ticket properly punched, I move on to the sensibilities of the people in that underworld. How many are atrophied from childhood, how many blunted in transit to the grave (to the Tombs? Isn't there a prison in the city called the Tombs?) and how many have sensibilities just as fragile and exposed as mine?

Does it matter how many? Doesn't the question concern rather whether it is conscionable that a psychologically sophisticated society, such as ours must admit to have become, can hold down in place by the flat of its hand a vast administrative apparatus designed to blot out in a tawdry routine way the uniqueness of every human being, processee or processor? It's the flat of *our* hand that holds this thing in place. We don't know what to say or how to do anything else. Like Balaam and other unwilling prophets, we seem moved to say and do our allotted parts whether we will or no. But prophet is not a good word. We have no vision. That's our trouble, that our imagination was tailored, trimmed, and finished to assess and reform human conditions of a Dickensian quality, but we are living in an America now where human conditions are Kafkaesque, and we on our side can't encompass them.

But the young encompass them this way: that there are two hundred million people in this country, this land of the free, and the number we are *now* enabling, through the democratic process, to pass their lives with human dignity is almost nearly possibly none. This is surely new. Three quarters of us affluent; four quarters living in an inconsonant ethical climate; those of us in charge, the establishment, incapacitated from responding to things as they really are because our moral senses were tuned to hear platitudes and respond with platitudes, to see human misery and to legislate for its removal—time and time again to legislate the removal of human misery.

And we have socked away this vast capital of social legislation and are indisputably rich in progress, from all of which evidence the young turn resolutely away, blind to it, deaf to it. With their senses conditioned in a psychological age, they look only at the two hundred million people— nearly one by one they tick them off—to reveal what manner of man the American Way of Life is producing.

And we are not insensitive. So far is that from the truth that, were we to switch attention from legislating the removal of human misery to "that very fact of frequency" in which men are distraught, violated, morally maimed, it would be to us like hearing the grass grow and the squirrel's heart beat, and our frames could hardly bear much of it.

How can *their* frames bear it? The revolution is already completed for this new breed, and they are not political man, confident reformer, but psychological man, extraordinarily sensitized to this frequency of tragedy. How can their frames bear it? The answer, my friends, is blowing in the wind, the the answer is that the young are political reformers, too, of course, but with their insights scattered beyond the orderly boundaries of our New Deal world. This unrestraint in the matter of insight produces these rude non-negotiable demands and meanwhile releases outwards a tremendous lot of angry fury, which, were it repressed and inward, would indeed not be bearable, but this way is—exhilarating.

IX I, Carer

Here he struck himself upon his breast or moral garden.

Martin Chuzzlewit

We are too psychologically aware. I've said it three times now, and when you've used something three times it's yours. This is the vocabularly-building nostrum of my childhood and, good grief, there it still seems to be, sitting in a pile of homiletic litter on the floor of my mind. I will try to describe what this means to me, an old progressive, staggered by the implications; and what it means, on the other hand, to this new breed, the Smith girls and my own children, who are not progressive, who don't have our shattered illusions. They have illusions, of course.

In the Dickensian days of the New Deal we in America had reached a higher degree of communal sensitivity towards human misery than our Victorian (?) grandfathers had. We discovered that while the peerless Free Enterprise system certainly did seem to propel itself into the future, improving us in admirable arithmetic progression, it did so by a mean cyclical mechanism that flung us up and outwards into unparalleled prosperity and then, in an exacting Calvinist way, required us to pay for that prosperity by next flinging us down into an unparalleled depression. Those flung down hardest did not believe they had been dashed by the Whim of

Providence, a view which our ancestors found reassuring. Curious. They were dashed down by something defective in the peerless economic system, and joblessness and hunger were now unendurable human suffering, and presiding over my nation's conscience, handsome, noble Franklin D. Roosevelt knew what our obligations were.

A man without a job must have a job, a hungry man must be fed. Legislate that and you establish by fiat the dignity of man. The dignity of man was a right that was bestowable in much the way that, personally speaking, I was humbly able to bestow the dignity of woman on myself with the tap of my wand on my own head. That is to say, I wasn't able. "The selfish instincts are not subdued by the sight of buttercups," George Eliot wrote more than a hundred years ago. "To make men moral something more is requisite than to turn them out to grass." Well, I didn't know that. Or perhaps it would be more accurate to say that I didn't allow myself to know that.

I certainly didn't know that you can't bestow dignity, that the most you can aspire to is an Act of Enablement, a legislative term that I find oddly tender. (Very odd indeed since it derives, I am told, from the decree that secured Hitler his power.) And something much less complicated that I didn't know was that the concept of social welfare and social responsibility towards the hapless victims of the economic cycle was not a brand-new generous notion quite typically thought up in the American mind, where all generous and progressive and true ideas were generated. Did I ever hear of Bismarck's reforms, of what England and Scandinavian societies had already effected in this line? Had I the least inkling that we were not in the vanguard but quite the contrary, pontificating, huffing and puffing from the rear, and that the best that could be said about our New Deal was that it was about time? If I had been told that in those countries where new deals had already been dealt, it was not only the poets who suffered a depression of spirit, not only the poets who seemed sunk by the heavy determinism in individual human suffering appearing nearly impossible to leaven, I would not have believed it, could not have, and to some extent *will* not to this day.

The New Deal, by Dickensian logic, ought to have become the mechanism which released the better man, let each one spring into the free, democratic, ethical, responsible, and ultimately cultured citizen that the soul yearns for the self to become, and I don't fully disbelieve this either, that the soul yearns upward. And I subject this view to the same sharp criticism George Eliot directed to Dickens, otherwise to her "the great novelist," that he encouraged "the miserable fallacy that high morality and refined sentiment can grow out of harsh social relations, ignorance, and want; or that the working-classes are in a condition to enter at once into a millennial state of altruism, wherein every one is caring for every one else, and no one for himself."

Perhaps we can take the measure of our predicament now by watching how far we are receding from that millennial state of altruism, of wide caring, widest caring, always remembering that caring is a state of mind and heart which is incubated by anybody's mother's warm arms and warm breath, but which must in the grown man be brought to a condition of useful responsibility and kept there by a lifetime's journey of the imagination through all human pain and irony. Today a qualified carer who first takes his morning *Times'* guided tour through Nigeria, Biafra, Belfast, Northern Mississippi, Prague, or whatever is that day's geography of despair has much too much ground to cover, and still he won't run across the state of Altruism, and doesn't expect to. He knows long since that high morality and refined sentiment cannot grow out of harsh social relations, ignorance, and want, a condition that covers nine-tenths or more of the earth's people, and that high morality and refined sentiments aren't growing in the other tenth, the affluent middle class, but are blighted there, too, are eaten by a brown rot, the consequence of ecological disturbance and mental disturbance, both. And yet all over the world there is evidence that in some young high morality is flourishing, although the case for refined sentiment would be harder to win—alive, if not flourishing, I would say.

When I was a schoolgirl, were you to learn that children were starving in Mississippi, why you would be shocked and care very deeply, and support a free milk program, and satisfy your altruistic needs, and legislate against misery, give them a *new deal.* But a real carer today takes a dismal path (which he follows "like a tedious argument of insidious intent") that is not very satisfying at all to his altruistic needs. These starving Mississippi children, malnourished even *in utero,* will have had their brain cells irreversibly underdeveloped, just as their bodies are stunted, for lack of the timely minimal nourishment necessary for the formation of brain and body. Gather to your breast the implications of that. But anyhow, I, carer, throw my whole weight behind any going plan to feed these people, double the food stamps, *triple* the food stamps, reap my satisfaction from those statistics at the end of the year which announce that the daily allotment of free food per qualified needy person has increased *three hundred percent,* from four cents per diem to twelve. And that twelve cents, moreover, is high protein, protein wrested from the grasp of Agricultural Interests whose single anxiety was to be benevolent out of their surplus of starches.

It is a characteristic of the New Deal mind that it derives marvelous comfort from percentage points, and it is a characteristic of this new young generation that it doesn't derive any comfort whatsoever from them. And I mention as an aside that this may account for a certain odd uselessness about sociology, a discipline that is so steeped in the study of human misery that you would think all its resources would be pored over and hoarded by the young for directing any of its three revolutions. But even I have sometimes had such a sense that there is a lesser gulf between me and Warren G. Harding than the one across which I converse uneasily with a handsome sociologist I know. "Listen here, Cynthia, you simply can't ignore these figures, this increase of *three hundred percent.*" I simply can. I am useless to his sociology with my unstatistical emotions, and I turn him off.

Now that the New Deal has become a historical era (a possibility it had been so hard for me to entertain) it is the subject of most patronizing criticism, but I don't read about that, and I don't want to contribute to it. After all, it is unfair, because to indict the New Deal for the simple black-and-whiteness of its vision is anachronistic. Nobody knew then, for instance, that malnutrition in the mother could damage the fetal brain, and it was a jarring surprise to us when we learned this just a few years ago. Why it was a surprise is an interesting question. And, likewise, until just a little time ago there was in my puzzle of understanding the unexamined assumption that psychologically speaking, the really poor, the underclass, did not have neuroses. Neuroses were an affliction of the middle class. You had to have time to cultivate them, you had to have the leisure. The poor did not have time, were forever needing to scramble after the means merely to stay alive. This scramble could drive them insane, but then they were psychotic, not neurotic. Well, and then a really extensive study was made of impoverished people packed in hot slums, and it seems that they are very liable to be severely depressed by their lot, that so rarely can they negotiate with society for bearable terms of existence that they tend to be paranoid, that the maleness of the man is badly undermined by his impotence in most matters, and the woman's confidence is likely to have been subverted. That they make terrible parents. That the children born into that sort of environment have characterological troubles galore. And it is an interesting question why this should be a surprise too.

Surprising or not, these psychological dimensions were not factors in the hard knowledge of social problems in the 30s and 40s. The hard knowledge was that President Roosevelt saw "one-third of a nation ill-housed, ill-clad, ill-nourished." You give these people a new deal—and notice what flames in the very spirit of that term *new deal,* a card-playing term, and not only a card-playing term but a specifically American card-playing term which carries in the new dealing a vision of open frontiers in the West, a defiance of fate, the promise of another chance, better luck in the land of the free will, where determinism is a depressing and unpatriotic force: and in my girlhood, a force, like violence, whose existence was not recognized.

Now on the wings of this sense of surprise I would like to retraverse the flight path I must have taken from political to psychological creature, from the New Deal land where the hungry are fed *tout court,* and you legislate against human misery and move perceptibly on towards that millennial state of altruism which has always been the American destiny, to now. It was explained to me once that when you are a patient in psychoanalysis it may happen to you that in the course of treatment you suddenly experience the most enormous insight, the most startling, surprising, and fantastic shock of knowledge, and you reel out of your hour in a stunned state, the whole of life abruptly seen through adjusted lenses, and the next day this insight has disappeared along with the astonishment and surprise into the compendium of assorted truths that you always knew, and becomes another truth that you always knew, that you cannot unknow. So you are left more or less with surprise at your sensation of surprise.

When I was an undergraduate I was a believer in progress, progress catapulting wildly on, an ameliorating force, kept smartly in line by good social legislation, but inside the politically responsible citizen that this view made me, there was conflicting, unamendable, stubborn disbelief that the sight of buttercups will suffice to subdue men's selfish instincts. I suppressed this disbelief. When you arrive at Smith

devoted to Ameliorating Progress, it is to some extent comparable to arriving at Smith a firm Southern Methodist or a
Westchester County Republican, except that the very lustiness
of your age, of being eighteen and twenty, keeps you sanguine
and cheery, keeps the doubts well buried, and meanwhile you
are being joined and fortified by the church-leavers and the
new New Dealers. The disbelief in the efficacy of buttercups
wells up later, when you are older, quickened by the series
of those enormous surprises over news that you always knew
about the complicated psychological givens in each human
being.

These surprises pricked me when I was thirty, thirty-five,
forty and will for life, no doubt, but Tony, Julie, Maggie,
and even Jenny, children nurtured by the 60s, have grown
in psychological awareness concomitantly with every other
awareness. They learn about the connection between under-
nourishment and damaged brain cells when I do, from the
same day's *Times,* or more likely, from Walter Cronkite.
They are distressed beyond measure, sensitive and feeling
and kindly children that they are, but they aren't *depressed.*
I would like to make the point that you might well have had
to have been a progressive in order to resign in despair now.
This new breed is not doctrinaire progressive. If I, coming
from my sanguine past, have to gather the implications day
after day of, first, the great sweeping disasters of Vietnam
and racism; and, then, this endless evidence of subtler but
not necessarily less excoriating violation to ordinary man, like
too little protein for the brain cells in Mississippi or Biafra
(in whole continents and sub-continents) or what happens to
you when you protest against conditions on the Long Island

Railroad, then the one thing that is not surprising is that there is effected an erosion of my satisfaction in all that Measurable Progress, all those Landmarks in Legislation.

They have no program. "What is most impressive about the revolutionary fervor in America today," says Henry Steele Commager in an angry swing against the young in honor of the Fourth of July, "is its negative and destructive character." Not like 1776 one bit. Not like us, the progressive reformers. We had a program. Just for example: we worked very hard to pass all those labor laws that would enable *all* Americans to take up "high morality and fine sentiment." Very hard, and through the democratic process, and for long years, we worked. But if I look at the unions now, and the sort of man a union man is, and what he thinks, and how his selfish instincts are doing, then I believe that ours might well have been a program for the theater of the absurd.

The revolutionary fervor as it produces outbursts that are violent or scatological sends me down to the bottom with a thud. I record the depression readily enough. I acknowledge an underlying comic despair that keeps us laughing on this east end of Harrison Avenue as we drift towards evening at our middle-aged leisure to one porch or another and drink something together. (And there must be a conduit running with cheap American red wine through the rear of these houses, because that is what I'd rather drink, and it's always in good supply, and I drink it in good faith on the assumption—not really too closely examined, this one—that the California strike is about *table* grapes and I am not breaking the boycott.)

Still, what is most impressive to me about the revolutionary fervor in America today is its exhilarating character. I am exhilarated, but not by those mad close-minded zealots, Maoists, Cheists, negritudinists, sexists, more ists with their isms. They boggle me, leave me incredulous before such naïveté. It is the open mind of that new breed that automatically, effortlessly encompasses, easily lives with and honors the psychological complexity, integrity of every single damn human being (outside the middle class), making it absolutely impossible, I would think, to embark upon any scheme whatsoever the aim and ambition of which would be to improve the sum total of human happiness on even only sixteen square blocks in Harlem, let alone something geographically larger, like a region or a country or a continent.

They have no program. They cut right through the infrastructure of administration to face people who need them, one to one. That's what our Smith senior is doing, turning her back upon my dear college community without a tear, without a thought, off to become one of the world's worst alumnae, direct to a ghetto classroom, where she intends to suffuse with the joy of music each one of eighty-seven third-grade children. That is her challenge and that will be her satisfaction (now, at the moment). And similarly, our most admired Doctor of the Cinema, who is leaving us with most breezy good will, is abandoning for a couple of years any orthodox, pinpointable plan for the pursuit of a career, to take on human relations catch as catch can, without even an institute grant to certify his importance.

So that is what those two will do to increase the sum total of human happiness on this teeming planet, and that, I suspect, is the direction our own girls will take, too. It is certainly different from the kind of thing I flung myself into. I've led a very busy useful life under my citizen's hat. I was up and doing all along. And I can look back and can't even remember the causes I supported, the contributions in time and money I've made, for labor in the old days, through to civil rights legislation in the new, always fighting the good fight—and always, it was a pretty good show. And all that is true. I don't subscribe to the cynical notion that it was nothing, gossamer.

How does the account stand? Suppose I pause now to see, after all that, how appreciably the sum total of human happiness has increased?

X   I, Endurer

I believe in aristocracy . . . if that is the right word and if a democrat may use it. Not an aristocracy of power based upon rank or influence, but an aristocracy of the sensitive, the considerate and the plucky. Its members are to be found in all nations and classes, and all through the ages, and there is a secret understanding between them when they meet.

E. M. FORSTER

I run my mind back to that frail woman, Smith '03, with her fine delicate nose bones and cheek bones, a good classical head for a good classical mind, making the best alumna; and forth to Joanne, Smith '69, setting out joyously in her beautiful solid flesh and black-brown eyes, to make the worst—sixty-six years between them and I falling somewhere nearer to the present; the old woman with her justified impatience saying, "They will not allow for time!" and archetypal Joanne, the Now Girl, and I, swung partway across the arc of life between them, hung up by this question of time.

There are injustices in the world and grievances in the college, and for the young they are a call to arms, and for the old they are a call for suitable policies devised for the rectification of the large wrongs and the small, through democratic channels and procedures, taking time. What is time for Joanne? The past is discredited. The present is now. And the future is now, in transit, clipping along. For the best alumna, the wisdom of age is contained in this: "You must allow for time to adjust these 'discrepancies,' and meanwhile you must endure them." And I interpolate. Endurance is excellent self-discipline. Life is full of frustrations, and the better you are at enduring the taller you become. Sitting through long Sunday-morning sermons in childhood is the lesson that enables you the better to sit through lectures at college. (But our children have not had to sit through long sermons; they have not had to do what they have not wanted to do. So they are very bad endurers.) Units of Endurance are the building blocks for character, a character so singularly disciplined that it seems often to seek its gratification in a lifetime's attendance record at lectures, talks, addresses at meetings, classes, clubs. That is what educated American women have been doing for character growth. When I sit through a lecture without my knitting and don't wriggle, I feel my character grow.

What a queer thing it is to love endurance for its own sake without asking whether it is reasonable to honor the thing you are enduring with your endurance, but that is what I was trained to do. So then I plough myself backwards again between the snowbanks of the lovely campus I remember through a girl's eyes, wondering about whether I was aware of enduring discrepancies, and all at once I find myself in a winter landscape full of them. And I begin to brood over now one and now another until I've worked myself into a mad state of delayed agitation. I'm suddenly stirred by a welter of remembered retrospective grievances and about that chronic state of submission in which I lolled through them.

I have difficulty settling on a prototype.

Just days ago I could have said, Oh what a lovely college and how I loved it (and it was true) and left my four years undisturbed, and be left with just some more lines of Prufrock sliding, sliding through other thoughts.

(Would it have been worth while
To have bitten off the matter with a smile,
To have squeezed the universe into a ball
To roll it toward some overwhelming question. . . .)

I make no criticism of the curriculum, because as a student I thought I was fully unqualified to judge, and twenty years later I see that I was one hundred percent right there—my best score. I do remember complaints about the foolish use-lessness of our liberal arts training, since when we left Smith we were as unemployable as when we entered, having learned no trade. But I discount this reasoning. Last year I sat next to a junior at a lecture who said, "Well, I'm majoring in English but I often wonder whether it isn't a mistake and I ought to be in Government," and I leapt in with my passion for making everything be all right and told her that it doesn't matter what you are *reading* in. And I told her that I thought of my own mind as beginning, embryonic, inside a round encasement very like a head, and wrapped up, *emballé,* balled up in infinite layers of filmy illusion, and that I read and married and read and had babies, and layer by layer the illusions burst and peeled off, and looking out from the inside I see increasingly more clearly what is ethically and intellectually tenable, and that's what happens when you read, and you read on until you're dead and that's life. She has been born layers closer to reality and so did or did not see me clearly, and did or did not think, Madam, you are off your trolley. But I worry about their not reading, the new breed.

We read, but whether the courses were more "relevant" to our times than is so today, I don't know. To wonder about the relevance of *anything* then, would have led me towards an overwhelming question, and I didn't wonder. Courses, content, requirements will always need altering, and academics are more liable to an intellectual arrogance which produces rigidity, than say cheerleaders, and more entitled to it, and this is as true in the social sciences as in the classics. Truer. So there is a terrible sluggishness about rationalizing the curriculum by rational means, and I doubt that three revolutions together can pry a believing man's mind from his obsessive principles.

I arrived on that campus at eighteen with a head wrapped on the outside with illusions, containing inside a clutter of little moralisms, and there never was a time through the four years of my residence that I caught a glimpse of the interconnection of all learning, but the fault was in me and not with Smith. I was a healthy bright American girl with the moralisms jockeying around in my brain to serve this or that purpose, or more usually, being jockeyed out of the way of impeding this or that purpose. Inside the classroom I listened, doodled, ate Hershey bars, fantasied about sex, teachers, boys, men, love, and synonymous subjects. It is the extracurricular vapor that, I see all at once, was so chillingly inhospitable to growth. Outside the classroom the demands made by bombast and trivia upon one's time for reflection were monumental, and the reason hardly anybody remembers to protest in retrospect is that they were so weightless as to remain nearly unrecorded in one's memory.

Outside the classroom was gym. I considered using the two years of required physical education in order to examine my capacity for endurance, but I am going to use student government instead. Still, I did think required gym was an intolerable demand, and I was reawakened to my old outrage by my neighbor's daughter, a freshman this year, who came hallooing down the street yesterday afternoon—barefoot, psychedelic bellbottoms, great felt sombrero—and paused to announce, "I've just had a written would you believe in badminton?" Oh grand delicious idiocy, wasn't it just as idiotic for me, and didn't I think so? Yes, I thought so. I thought the trivial indignities to which my resolutely untrim body was subjected were inspired by minds so irrational as to be unencompassable by a person like me. Me playing hockey, me folk dancing, me doing archery, me always nearly flunking: talk about what was weary, stale, flat, and unprofitable, and it was my association with the physical education department. The whole thing would have faded irretrievably, were it not for the unfadable memory of an intimate little conference you had once in your freshman year and once in your senior year over your Posture Pictures. These posture pictures were black-and-white silhouettes of your naked profile, head to foot, and you discussed with your teacher, she pointing at your swayback or your belly with her pencil, the improvement over four years, or in my case the lack of improvement over four years (and you are now twenty-one), of your *posture,* for goodness' sake. To be made to stand stripped, naked, bare, exposed, helpless before that camera twice, afterwards to examine that terrible black indictment with a certifiable pencil-poking fanatic is an experience I probably would not otherwise easily have come by.

Now for student government, which is my real case study, and which I choose on account of the recent discovery on the campuses that this representative American institution in miniature, this bicameral legislature under a federal system, this fake, properly brought into focus, was typical of collegiate banality, was form without content, parliamentarian exercises over trivia, not for grownups, and that's what I thought a quarter of a century ago. When I was an undergraduate I ran for office only once and only for personal glory, and otherwise regarded our democratic polity and its works as a totally ignorable bore. Yet there it was, all blown up with significance, taking up a large space in the panorama of Fine Things, standing like a structural pillar before your view in the theater, when you were vaguely waving your head around to see what was really going on, what mattered and what didn't. There were lots of pillars like that all around life, '44–'48.

I traveled in a most sophisticated, superior, unworshipful, chapel-cutting, selectively misbehaving roving band that decided, being a tight clique with some government majors, that it would be very funny to make me the president of our dormitory. So, doing what a well-organized minority does when it takes the scattered majority unawares (two of these government majors were Phi Beta Kappa, but not I, of course), they ran me and won me.

I then somersaulted. So immersed was I in the mystique of honor associated with high office that I dropped my mockery and turned into an earnest people's servant faster than Prince Hal, except more uneasy lied my head. This reversion engaged me in some queer ethical maneuvers which I'm afraid, in all their appalling pettiness, must nonetheless be recognized as the parallel of large, anguishing moral dilemmas that I know lacerate many sensitive students today. We are friends of a Radcliffe girl who was torn miserably between her personal judgment, which was to vote no to a strike, and her sense of betrayal towards her dear friends and promoters. Well, I was miserably torn as Mme Presidente between joining my friends in swiping the leftover pie from the dormitory kitchen, as was our wont, and besmirching the trust inherent in my office. (So I went with them but I didn't eat the pie, and I must testify to the fine quality of my friends that they never regarded my dilemma or my solutions with anything more respectful than affectionate contempt.)

Have I, in this chance recollection, hit upon a beautiful symptom of our generational malaise, which was that all our ethical principles were exercised in microcosm, in little? My conscience, for instance, was always asked to do battle in a small, petty, meager, trifling, inconsequential conflict which stood in for a major conflict in the real world. The four undergraduate years were rehearsal, and every extracurricular thing was a mock-up, and I was right to mock. And if there was a lesson at all that I learned from that particular conflict about the pie, it was that I should have eaten it. The benefit to my character, the character of my friends, the college, society at large was zero, nothing.

And this indignation that I feel as I sit here poking ancient sores does not derive from an idea that we were deliberately flummoxed, that the whole thing was a put-on, that the policy of the college and the country emanated from a crafty intention to distract you from entertaining any revolutionary notions or getting pregnant. Craftless, guileless, everybody was. But *regardez* what the Smith College House of Representatives was attending to in my time to make you fine little citizens; little citizens when you were able to and ought to have become big citizens. An enormous outsized experience in the art of compromise, patience, endurance, good democratic things, derived from a lathering debate about moving the closing hour of the dormitories on Friday nights from eleven-thirty to midnight. It was finally so moved. Exhausted, needing to reconstitute, revitalize ourselves before tackling Saturday night, facing bravely the fact that there were seven nights to a week and only one reckoned with, but each of them calling for justice, we then tackled on, and . . . my recollection is that the process took care of my four years of Democracy at Work, but then I really was very inattentive, and recollection may not serve.

For those four years, outside the classroom, we lived life In Little. I did not doubt the honesty of those dedicated to a policy of making everything nice and small, but I felt myself a great big grown-up girl forever being expected to take seriously a lot of silly things, and half-consciously, I didn't. To the extent that I thought about the ludicrous assortment of miniature lessons served up as real life to capture my extracurricular energies, to that extent I thought it was a ludicrous assortment. My energies went to fending them off. What I couldn't evade, I endured.

We learned to be great endurers, a credit to the college if

that was really what it was after, endurers beyond the most sanguine hopes of the oldest alumnae. It was a bad thing, an eroding process. For we are back now to the problem of what happens to large, full-grown women, altogether as ready emotionally and intellectually as my girls are to comprehend macrocosmically, when they are forced to play out the role of innocence and they are not innocent.

We are back to two different things. The first is the evidence of this discrepancy between how childish was society's assessment of eighteen- and twenty-year-old women, and how mature were their actual needs, intellectual and ethical. We were stretched unbelievably far across this descrepancy. The second is that one can turn up some assumptions that upon examination remain feasible through young adolescence (Maggie, stand up straight!—which I don't actually say in the sublime hope that after ten years of hearing it she will suddenly become convinced of the soundness of my order) but turn ridiculous when they are scientized and made into an assault upon the private precincts of the self of a slumpy full-grown woman.

Take *mens sana in corpore sano*. How grand this classical balance and how rare—right? Can you impose it on an unwilling adult? Get out there and move your blooming bottom! Can you impose it on an unwilling child? Or is his inclination to be thus balanced settled in those first five years, *in utero* included, assigned by Dr. Dubos? Not that splendid praise should not go to the mother who gets her unathletic girl to join the Y swimming team because it is hard to do and goes against everything in my experience (but I am taking us as a point of reference, and it is possible we are extraordinarily sluggish as a family, more than possible). Splendid praise should! At what age these parental efforts may be abandoned in fair conscience must vary. Some time during adolescence it begins to seem vindictive to make a resistant individual go through the motions. In fact, as the Now mother of Now children, I see that a point arrives in the mid-teens, earlier than college age, when it becomes an unnatural act to continue to manage or direct, or guide, or even manipulate some kinds of activities and some kinds of responses in your child or anybody else's where earlier, in his younger days, it was the healthy stabilizing responsible thing for one to do.

I expect, when presented to a sound-mind-healthy-body striver, to admire his physical condition, or anyway to acknowledge it, but I don't expect to admire how well his intellect weighs in the balance, although it happens. The old idea of balance no longer seems to be a human attribute after all. It was based in the normal man, valued by the average man. But in the psychological age how do you begin to draw a balance from the rich confusion that anybody is? Balance is not a precise and useful word, not a *deep* word, any more, just as normal isn't, and the average man has disappeared.

The paternalism at Smith when I was there was only a mildly violating feather-brushing of my sense of adult integrity, since I lived within the framework of that picture-puzzle life that was my world. We submitted endlessly to negotiations for the recognition of our full womanhood, by the democratic process, as, for instance, through that struggle for an extra half-hour of vulnerability to sexual temptation Friday nights. My daughters, meanwhile will have recognized in themselves the fullness of their womanhood by the time they leave this house to go to college, and it will be a revolution already accomplished in the way they see themselves. So if they land on a campus where this recognition is denied by the administration, why, the Julie and Maggie we love and respect have no alternative but to regard this recognition as a non-negotiable demand (courteously and peacefully demanded). They can't un-be what they are.

Now it may be said reasonably that my grand defense of the maturity of this new breed depends upon carefully overlooking the preponderant numbers who are very immature. But I overlook immature people of forty and fifty. I don't argue that maturity is present at eighteen, but that it is appropriate, with today's biological and intellectual and psychological givens, to expect it to be present. And under the circumstances of these givens the policy of the grudging piecemeal delivery of "rights" to the students ought to be thrown up, and a tripartite committee, or whatever is most mod in the participatory democracy line, should begin clean in this world without time, to draw up new rules for life in a mature community of scholars. I'll draw them up, if they like: I love that community. It should be a fit place for E. M. Forster's aristocracy of the sensitive, the considerate and the plucky.

XI *Autonomy*

Strange, that some of us, with quick alternate vision,
see beyond our infatuations, and even while we rave
on the heights, behold the wide plain where our persistent self pauses and awaits us.*

GEORGE ELIOT

Jenny was three when our last child was due to be born, and
it somehow came about in our preparing the way for its
welcome that each of the children volunteered to take on
some part of its training. Jenny said she would teach it to
share. When I came home from the hospital and put Nora
in her arms, the others asked cheerfully, "What about the
sharing, Jenny?" and Jenny lifted her sweet head, nearly lifted
an eyebrow, and gave a little nod of acknowledgment which
implied, as to the sharing, it was probable there would be a
delay in the need for her services.

So thoroughly do we rear our children by lending them
little slips of adult wisdom, letting them try on parental
authority, pretend to mature responsibility, by bringing all
life's lessons down to their size, that we are rarely aware of
the mechanism. I was a little aware of the mechanism when
I noticed that it wasn't operating where it used to, with playing house. Jenny and Nora never played house very much.
They never hugged baby dolls. I would gratify a great welling

119

urge in myself by having baby dolls under the tree for them, and tea sets and doll carriages. I crocheted a beautiful blanket for Nora's doll's crib while I waited with my mother through the three days until my father's funeral, and I was touching deep strains in myself, but the blanket was not really needed. I am a domestic female, not only a cooking and baby-cradling but a cotton-starching and silver-polishing variant of which there are not many left, and it's curious that the two little ones fail to play house along my lines. So many other lines cross mine out, lines fused by these revolutions, and I suppose that if I follow my own thesis, Nora and Jenny's female identity must be moving firmly towards a destiny more complex, sophisticated, and I believe, ethically responsible than what my childhood was intending me to become. This thesis, however, will have to contend with a lot of disorderly facts, as, for instance, that I was a great house-player in my childhood but not possibly on account of emulation. Even once to have seen her wash dishes would have seemed to me a disturbing misuse of my mother.

What I have become is an individual matter. Still if the best of the young are willfully unorthodox in their patriotic and religious and familial behavior, never to return to the old ways, the schism derives from us, the parents. That is why I have needed to look back at myself, to bear witness to my college years where the discrepancy between what we were given and what we could take was overstretched, where real life continued to be kept at bay, and the learning process naturally evolved from playing house and playing mother to playing democracy and playing citizen. Finally this discrepancy must have been schismatic. After all, these revolutions are religious wars fought over the interpretation of our oldest moral principles: love thy neighbor, thou shalt not kill, all men are created equal.

For us at Smith the Microcosm, the strain on our powers of credulity and submission was exhausting, and those temperamentally able to believe, those who were orthodox, traditional, in the main body of the church, moved on from the atypical peace and goodness of campus life to marry and bear children as the scenarists prescribed, to strive in their houses, on their blocks, in their neighborhoods to have everything atypically peaceful and good there, too. Having learned too well to look at life in little, to make believe that the impositions upon one's time and mind, antiseptic or trivial or artificial as they seemed, were real and signified, and being especially fine endurers, they could readily continue to play citizen and then parent at suburban PTAs, Scouts, Medical Wives Auxiliaries, where all the problems were small, unrepresentative, and unreal.

Outside, the world was coming to its wits' end. I often wondered then what an educated young woman made of the American political scene, which was dominated by the always surely intellectually discreditable notion that we were being encircled by an International Communist Conspiracy—how, having sat in those Smith classrooms at least, she could still, anyway, join the Young Republicans for Eisenhower. Why, under thirty as she was, would she not rise up in revolt against such insipidity? Well, she was not a political revolutionary. And she could sit in a morally unresponsive church, never hearing that God was black, not needing revolution in religion. She didn't balk as a student and as to her sense of femaleness, I can't imagine what anybody else's sexual identity was when we were in our twenties, so shy was I about my own.

So there were those three revolutions, already heating up in their several ways, and there were the rapidly accumulating data on racial injustice, overpopulation, environmental pollution, the martial and political consequences of fear and hysteria in domestic and foreign affairs, and there was this young Smith graduate trying to do the right thing by going to the PTA in a school where all the children were white and middle class. And she came home exhausted from it. I did it, and it is exhausting. She had been taught to think small, and I suppose she thought small, and supported the whole apparatus of small thinking, which was the unbreached American establishment to about 1960.

Her children are probably revolutionaries anyway, or smoking pot and dropping out. Scarlett O'Hara, who disliked anything disagreeable, said in the movies, if memory serves, "I won't think about that today. I'll think about that tomorrow." What percentage of my classmates, when just over thirty, gathered for their tenth reunion at Smith (1958) registered non-thinkers, I wouldn't guess, but whatever they weren't thinking about went on anyway. And none of us has remained immune. By the twentieth reunion it was clear we were all undermined. The small thinker, the woman who stayed in the mother church, lived with the discrepancy stretching on and on, the inherent structural weakness subverting her positions as mother, woman, believer, citizen.

As to the big thinkers like me, I've already said we didn't do any good. We graduated from Smith and scattered. We were early schismatics, unorganized, proliferating into innumerable little sects, but we shared a distinguishing protestant mark. However much we varied in the lives we led and the mothers we made, we were all assailed by Doubt: and this was better than not being assailed by doubt, given the substance of what we had been required to believe. Our children were permissively reared (and by ours, I don't mean mine), and learned their moral righteousness from us, and in fact learned all the things that we now know the Now Generation knows, from us, by intention, or by inadvertence.

I refer back once more to Bernard Bailyn's insight into the American Revolution—that it had already occurred in the colonial mind before the first shots at Concord—in order to discover traces of the already-occurred sexual revolution in the family, because, after all, the family is where sex is housed. If nothing else, doubt has dampened things at the hearth, and once you doubt you can't un-doubt, just as once you know, you can't un-know, and once you are you can't un-be. Here again I can only attempt to document, if one can fairly use such a notarizing word for such an irrational process, the evolution of myself as parent from Tony's birth in 1950 until today when Nora, our smallest (though roundest) child is eight.

We think of ourselves, my husband and I, as having begun our parenthood conservative and unpermissive, defending our clearing of civilization in the midst of a forest of savages (our dear friends and their children, the savages), and proceeding through these twenty years together in abiding love and harmony, never more lovingly harmonious than in our fierce and elemental resistance to permissivism, which we have viewed as a self-condemned fad, destined to a short life. I suppose, and now I will not speak for him any more, that I have always believed that one assumption that was going to stay immutable was the assumption that the way we brought up our children was the right way.

The conservative right way takes an essentially hierarchical view of life and at that crucial point is antithetical to the permissive, which is mindlessly egalitarian and has made the new breed, whatever else they are, levelers. I'm leveling off. I would have been ready to avow that in all things maternal I would remain unswerving and unswervable, but after all, layers and layers of righteousness have peeled from me, and it seems to be the case that a revolution has already been accomplished in me, the mother, too, and that practically unawares, if I overlook my counterinsurgency at Tony's guerrilla skirmishes, it has happened without a struggle. I still cannot abide ill-mannered children, and by good manners I mean to include at least as many rules specifically intended to refine and define and *confine* children as the stanchest lover of adult society can think up. Our house, and even this end of Harrison Avenue, is still a sanctuary from the wildlife all around, this being an academic community, and young academics tending themselves to be the new breed fully fledged, and their little children, the new, new, and to be avoided at any cost. My unbelieving self has lately had to relinquish with some dismay the assumption that permissivism in child-rearing was a short-lived fad.

I suppose by definition a conservative anybody is attached to a past something that he is determined to haul into the future, and thus easily regards himself as traversing through time: that is what I do. My childhood, not Draconian at all, was a tightly bridled passage for me as well as for any friend I had, perfectly designed to send my spirits lusting ahead to the future. My mother, who in many small things was relaxed and generous, still had to superintend my welfare according to the reigning wisdom, and my existence was dotted with social prohibitions, joys withheld or delayed, indulgences carefully measured, because the best things in life were not good for you when you were young. This put a tremendous premium on growing up, getting out, bolting; made adulthood seem divine, a time when you could eat pickles, ice cream, hot dogs, candy, soda pop, stay up all night, wear lipstick, silk stockings, high heels, earrings, and contradict, if not precisely your parent (ever), others. Respect was there, respect for power, but basically what adulthood represented was a vast repository of good things, morally good as well. I couldn't wait to get out and eat pickles and do fine things for humanity.

This hierarchical view, this sense of riding the time span up from childhood and out into the high skies of adult life, one's eyes fixed always on what's just beyond reach, is how I don't seem to be proceeding any more. But I was, in the early days of my motherhood still thus proceeding inexorably along this route, and I estimated and directed the growth of my children's development with a very long-range perspective concerning the effects I intended, a single-mindedness reminding me now somewhat of the process of drawing up a will with the best intentions towards the legatees, attempting to make reasonable provision to outwit future injustices, future mismanagement, and regardless of historical change.

Whoever has had anything to do with a nice fine will of that kind, in which all the original intentions are aborted, will notice that those psychologically complex human beings that the lawyers have converted into legal entities for the extremely rational and just distribution of the estate in question, many years later are still psychologically complex human beings, perversely unimproved into impassive legal entities.

I note that several meanings of the word "will" contain the intention to govern future human events, and I've relinquished these intentions. The future that occupies me has shrunk so that it is not so much farther away than our piano player's, a Now-in-transit. Time has changed for me from a simple strong arc on a line described from birth to death to a kind of post-impressionist cubist *Nude Ascending the Stairs* (and at the backside of the canvas, descending) because the present is both so complex and so compelling.

Here is this series of daughters for whom I have had the most conventionally exalted aspirations, grooming them from their babyhood to be acceptable to Smith, to Marry Well, to be ORNAMENTS (but ornaments to adorn what? to adorn whom?—I would have to let their sparkling glitter-to-be light that unknown and then look and see). I certainly wasn't grooming them for Princeton, to which school they may now well choose to apply. But suppose one or the other of them was acceptable to Princeton or Smith, would it ever have occurred to me in a flash of things to come that Princeton or Smith, having been tried and found wanting, might not, for goodness' sake be found acceptable to one of my girls? Never. It was not among the intellectual questions of my world to ponder that one: now it is.

I can be Janus, here. I can be my peers' protagonist for the liberal arts education. Follow it undeflected and in four years emerge discriminating in mind and heart. And I can watch today's undergraduate estimating the past success of the liberal arts education on the Pass-Fail system, marking it Fail. At Smith, Princeton *et alia,* where the pattern of the classical tradition was impressed like a cookie cutter on rolled-out dough, I have begun to look at a sample cookie from my batch with some scepticism. She should have had, this cookie, a large mind with a large view, but I have established for myself that she was diminished by graduation. In disproportionate numbers we were contracted, turned out small. It doesn't do to romanticize "the long solitary hours of library study" in the way that Princeton alumnus does, because what was the result of it? What did it make of him? The very reason for immersion in the humanities is to prepare you for rebirth into Forster's fine aristocracy of the mind, but it was not successful. Too rarely did the baptism take.

Looking either way, I can be adversary to either position. Yes, I am committed to the transcendent values of the classical discipline. No, I can't maintain that those values are being even approximately transmitted at that college to which we pay tuition, against the arguments of a daughter who may tell me they aren't.

And mind you, the classical discipline is a process of subdual. The words tell you that. Consider the entering freshmen welcomed with great exuberance to a really going revolution. How many will even hear that small classical voice calling for volunteers to be disciplined and subdued? Julie being the first of the girls to go off to college, we intend that she benefit from an excellent exercise in the honing of intellect, the refining of sensibilities. Merely subduing Julie will not be acceptable. Putting her down, as the young call it, *trying* to put down this quiet but extremely buoyant daughter, would exhaust the other side. I would have, before the revolutions, felt that to deliver oneself over willingly to four years of strict attention to this classical discipline, to retreat willingly for the benefit of oneself and the future benefit of humanity, was so obvious as to need no defense. Now, I think that it is the special need of some young to seek out a cloistered college. Otherwise, today, can one really reasonably attempt to persuade girls like ours to the logic of testing oneself for four years in ascetic, monastic seclusion? Can we ask them, really, to submit to a Smith '03 test of endurance? I think it would seem to them unethical, unnatural, grossly irresponsible, so conversant are they with the issues of this world, so early accustomed to include themselves among the people whose opinion counts and is counted, whose range of interests is as wide as mine, who have been exercised through their early teens by the implications of biological warfare, of biological welfare, who at twenty know George Eliot and T. S. Eliot (but in nothing like the way you know at forty). I may be Pollyanna C.P.S. Prufrock *ex.* Our girl is Julia Participatory Seton. She's off the drawing board. She is a beautiful fact. She isn't frivolous, or sexually bold, or insufficiently demure when she seeks out the grand mixture of at least two sexes in a spread of ages all the way to thirty at a coeducational institution that is spilling over into the streets like a Roman fountain, administered by people who can simultaneously weep for the passing of the old and listen carefully to the young and then say Yes and sometimes No.

It must be quite clear by now that the upheaval of this past decade upheaved me who would have subsided for life an extinct volcano of insignificant size, but it didn't up-heave my children. They weren't thrown up to the surface, they were born on it, evidently with the gift of levitation. But I wasn't, and as their pre-revolutionary mother, I got in my old-world licks, as you might say, before the cataclysm. And so through the first years that formed them, those years bracketed by Loyola and Freud and Dubos, our children were learning obedience in a stratified household with papa at the pinnacle, with no whining allowed, with piano lessons and good report cards, with great emphasis on not eating before dinner and saying how-do-you-do and other important things. And they grew up an amalgam. They breeze through this disregarding world with my rules of behavior, easily seeming to blend the double heritage, the way children in a bilingual family easily switch back and forth from French to English. They greet the chaos: and they keep their counsel. Not sample cookies out of the new batch, our girls. They're variables. We are all variables, probably the dearest fact of human life, forever having to be rediscovered and re-relished.

My husband and I struggled against being carried off by the great wave of permissivism in child-rearing that was swelling marvelously after World War II. I don't give us credit for being particularly discerning about children's needs for structure: it was our need for structure that was so de-termined. In any event, permissivism, in spite of us, became a tremendous cultish force, inviting a devotional adherence from people who had no other altars left. Today, among the new generation who are now in turn parents, it is not a cult.

When we are invited by younger people for eight-thirty (bad sign, no dinner) to meet this guy from Yale in anthropology who's moving up to McGill (bad sign, he is traveling with his family) over at the faculty apartments (very bad sign, a tribe that doesn't use sitters), we say we are so sorry but we'll be in Boston. This link with younger colleagues we like to keep broken. Still, sometimes there we are, glass in hand, in a mob scene conducted by children six weeks to about eight and a half years old, rocked and bumped and spilled on and spit up on ("Cynthia loves babies." "Yes, I do love babies, let me hold him"), feeling we are in a parlor George Price has drawn us in and left us stranded, and wondering why at nine, ten, eleven o'clock none of these children seems to get siphoned off to bed. They are not charming, warm, lovable, quiet, amusing little ones at this hour, not even their parents seem to think so, and these parents, I suspect, not altogether detached from Time, harbor a This-Too-Will-Pass relief clause in their contract with the Now. A case could be made for that first generation of permissive parents, that they really tended to be fanatics and ideologues. These people today, I sense, do not think they are dosing their young with panacea (the name for "the plant allheal, *obs.*"), but seem acquiescent and even depressed about the constant, unending abrasive presence of their young.

But it is impossible for them to live otherwise, impossible for them to think in hierarchical terms, to assign another human being a lesser place, with fewer rights and curtailed expression. They don't associate the idea of waiting, the grand principle of endurance, with character-building, but with what oppressed people have been piously counseled to do through history. ("For," as Mr. Pecksniff justly observed, "if every one were warm and well fed, we should lose the satisfaction of admiring the fortitude with which certain conditions of men bear cold and hunger. And if we were no better off than anybody else, what would become of our sense of gratitude, which," said Mr. Pecksniff with tears in his eyes, as he shook his fist at a beggar who wanted to get up behind, "is one of the holiest feelings of our common nature.")

These young parents, in short, are not hysterically certain that the formula they are using is foolproof, they are not mad zealots. They just know too much about repressive measures, and here again, one can't unknow. They must surely want their children to be worthy of that aristocracy of the sensitive, the considerate and the plucky to which they themselves belong. But consideration here runs smack into repression and is knocked flat. I yield before their dilemma. I'm glad it wasn't ours.

They live night and day in what I would have found unbearable, because interminable, intimacy with their children; and they remark, record, and store each moment of growth, as though there were no moral alternative to being such faithful monitors. What would happen if they looked away? Precious moments would be unrecorded, lost forever, a circuitous loss to the child, as if because his mother hadn't listened, his father wasn't bending over, his own private moments wouldn't count for him. So night and day they watch and tend minutely (and sometimes they of course do look away), and it is my observation from my friendships, that to the extent that the child is not repressed the parent is depressed. A mild and not-so-mild depression—and I don't use the word clinically but I do use it with compassion— characterizes the younger parents that I know, however else they differ from each other. I see that I have now said that they are not depressed politically, but they are parentally. I wonder whether this will hold?

Now I was repressed, but I was not depressed, I think. I say that I was role-playing, and that I was good at it. But role-playing is cover. Cheerful and on top of things as I seemed even to myself, I must record a constant, negative, threatening, amorphous shame which was beneath the surface of me, and this surface could at any moment be ripped away and I be laid bare, uncovered. If you are an actress, you recite, you read scripts, you are in interaction with an audience, you may miss your cue. My standing exposed, naked, outraged for that posture picture was really a graphic illustration of me stripped of cover, denied a role. I even see the association in my despair all these years later with those violated railway passengers. The shame has largely left me now, but the memory of it is no doubt the contributory force that causes me to exalt the revolutionary young in terms of their determined resistance to the violation of the self.

A while after Nora's birth, I recognize now, I had ceased to be all role-player responding to outside direction, and had become autonomous. That is why the littler girls didn't play house, probably. They've seen me ironing and cooking and tidying, fairly happily doing all that, but they see my performances as somewhat adjunctive.

XII Sacrifice

Yet he hath ever but slenderly known himself.
                                                    King Lear

Two copies of *Portnoy's Complaint* were circulating on our
block, and one landed in my lap the very day the *Times*
published the report that the Head Start program was a
failure. Well, I thought upon finishing both, sociologists the
world over, in drawing the portrait of the ideal mother-
substitute designed to rescue the drifting, neglected, unstimu-
lated, non-verbal, unmotivated, culturally deprived child,
might very well come up with Mrs. Portnoy. Could we but
harness her energies, her flair for invading the private
precincts of the soul (for she is the violating mother, arche-
typically) and every morning bus her, righteous and im-
placable, to the nearest black ghetto, surely even the most
phlegmatic little children with the smallest vocabularies
would be roused to defend their interior selves with every
weapon coming to mind, however polysyllabic. Just a thought.

  Mrs. Portnoy is merely an extreme case of what has happened through history when a certain sort of woman reads
the Fifth Commandment, Part B, HONOR THY MOTHER, as a
divine endorsement of her matriarchal rights based upon the
suspension of human fallibility in her particular case. This
seems to have been a fairly frequent phenomenon in which

sometimes whole societies conspired, and while I was never Portnoyesque, nor was my mother before me, it has not until recently struck me as an amazing presumption that a woman would feel herself automatically *entitled* to be gratified by what her son (or daughter) is and does as long as they both are living.

I'm not going to pursue Mrs. Portnoy for my purposes, because of her insistent semitism and the anti-semitism she evokes, both sides of a subject to my mind in every way overkilled. Instead I turn to Hardy's credible and dignified Mrs. Yeobright. When I reread *The Return of the Native* last spring I could not get over this fact about Mrs. Yeobright (it was to her house the mummers were going on Christmas Eve) that she felt herself automatically entitled to pass her life being gratified by the choices her son Clym made throughout his. She was felled by Clym's choice of Eustacia for his wife.

"How can he bear to grieve me when I have lived only for him all these years?" Mrs. Yeobright asks. But she asks in a lonely society in the remote southwest of England in about the year 1840: a timeless, changeless, hierarchical society in which her parental right is uncontested.

"It is the steady opposition in going wrong that he has shown," she says, unassailed by doubt that she can be in these matters the arbiter of right and wrong.

"I did not think one whom I called mine would grow up to treat me like this," saying "mine" easily, for all the assumptions pertaining to family love, gratitude, obedience were a hundred years from being examined—more than a hundred years in Wessex, probably.

"And this maternity—to give one's best years and best love to ensure the fate of being despised." Ah, but that is a cry that transcends the boundaries of historical change, a cry of unquenchable mother-pain enduring as childbirth. You hear it now in this rosy dawn of the psychological age, and I expect it will be heard into the future, if future there will be. But this one echoes back into the remote past, this cry from a woman whom Hardy describes as living on what may be "the very heath of that traditionary king of Wessex—Lear."

Honor thy father and mother. An alternate reading of the Fifth injunction of the Decalogue is that to bring order to this wild tribe of humans, to civilize these fractious nomads, it is Divine Wisdom to establish a hierarchical society based on the seniority system. It is this second reading I earlier leaned to. I still incline to a hierarchical arrangement of human affairs, but not one based on unearned honor.

When I lift my eyes to stare unseeing at the wall in front of me (upon which there are six framed pictures I care about), for some further illustration that the revolution has already occurred in me qua mother, I am impelled to repeat that the strongest assumption upon which ever I operated, the one least likely to have been subjected to my examination, was the assumption concerning the immutability of the maternal role. My mother was as immutable as Mrs. Yeobright; not like her, but as immutable. But lo, I have mutated. One of the framed pictures is of my father (who was pretty immutable, himself) taken at the first New York World's Fair (1940), "looking as if he were alive," a handsome, intelligent, articulate man, entirely prerevolutionary, whose mild voice I can nearly hear pronounce upon all this that I'm thinking now, "You're talking nonsense," his standard comment. (His father, my grandfather, would have said, "She's a damn fool," his standard comment). Next to that photograph is one taken a couple of years ago in Petticoat Lane, London, of our four girls cradling monkeys in their arms, their father presiding above them, gazing off, philosophical and a little wistful, and me. I love that picture of my husband, but is he wistful about his wife, the revolutionary? Directly in front of me is a wood engraving by Leonard Baskin of the funeral procession from *St. Julian,* a scene in a short story by Flaubert. It is a medieval tale about a young man whose love for hunting animals turns into an orgy of slaughtering them, and in a state of insatiable blood-lust he returns home to kill his mother and father by a terrible mistake. Then the penance (he walks on and on until he comes to a wide wild river, and there is no way to cross, and he makes himself the ferryman), and the final expiation. There is no horror comparable to parricide and no abnegation of the self comparable to Julien's expiation.

The legend of St. Julien is at once the passionate underwriting of the Fifth Commandment and its subversion; the seamless garment of familial love and obedience topside, and the ghastly tangled threads of fate (and hate and love) bottom. It is this theme which plays with the tension between the two generations that catches at my mind when I read now, though I never noticed it earlier. I watch for it, and by watching have had my hold loosened somewhat from the scruffs of my children's necks.

I suspect that a great emotional barrier to our understanding of the revolutionary proclivities of this generation is our platitudinous view of family. What we assume to be the normal, healthy, the *natural* relationship among fathers, sons, mothers, daughters is a condition of mutual and permanent love, respect and a readiness, and *appropriateness,* on the part of the parent to sacrifice himself for his child. This is what we think. It would be *unnatural* to think anything else. And it's not without a recognizable source, because I would be readily able to testify to a devotion to one's endangered child so intense as to make the willingness to sacrifice oneself unquestioned. But and however, this enormous sacrificing mother love which wells upward at critical moments should not be expected to maintain itself on that high devotional plateau throughout the workaday childhood of one's brood, and indiscriminately for life. Self-sacrifice is a position, it is perhaps too obvious to note, that implies reciprocity, a contract of mutuality which both are bound by, though only one has signed.

Meanwhile the balance tipped since Mrs. Yeobright's day. The gravitational shift in the family from parent-worship to child-worship in Western society is a fairly new development, as I read in a book recently, beginning for very good economical and sociological reasons towards the end of the seventeenth century, but we Americans don't know this. Devoted to the teleological idea that all previous history was but a gestation period for the birth of our nation, it is a fitting part of our national creed to believe there is something particularly American about motherhood, the kind of very fine thing that has been reserved for us to do. This national policy on mothers has left the family for a long time now in too tight a bind, and as it has gradually been psychologized for more sophisticated adaptation, the leading strings are pulled more taut than ever. The goad drives today's young mother to maintain a nurturing intimacy from which her off-spring is not gradually delivered at the termination of child-hood, and her challenge is to do it always with her hands held up wide open to show you that there really aren't any strings at all. Other kinds of women, not only the young but those my age and older, seem just goaded, not challenged. They may turn numb or mad.

For myself I am comforted by any evidence that mothers have been known to operate at a lower temperature. If I check off each relationship in my family I seem to see that keeping perpetually an insufficient distance one from the other would not have allowed the sense of autonomy of the self to take good hold in either, not in the parent, nor the child, not in the husband, nor the wife.

When one half-consciously listens, one may *over*hear. I was reading the autobiographical reflections of the Russian writer Aksakov in which he retells the story of *Beauty and the Beast* as he had heard it from his childhood nurse (ca. 1790). "There was a rich and famous merchant who had three daughters, all three sheer beauties, the youngest the loveliest of all, and he loved his daughters more than all his wealth. . . ." At the end of a long and exhausting journey he finds himself in thrall to the beast, "a kind of monster, terrible and shaggy-haired, which howled in a savage voice. . . ." This frightful creature promises to have him brutally torn apart unless he can persuade one of his daughters to be his ransom. He tries. Having been scared senseless, he races home and tries. He tries to persuade one after the other of

his young and lovely and beloved daughters to deliver herself body and soul to this unspeakably ghastly beast so that
he himself can live his life to the last possible moment. The
first two won't, but the third does gladly.

Here is an old tale appearing early in many parts of
Europe that is a testimony to unquestioned parental primacy
wherein our responses are singularly enlisted to admire the
sacrifice of the youngest daughter, to condemn the selfishness
of her two sisters, to entertain no negative thought about that
craven old man. Not that it isn't a fine story. My motive
merely is to disinter a homely attitude that prevailed in
Western society *before* the art of self-sacrifice had passed
from child to parent. And for those who are comforted by
the mutability of all things including parent-child relationships, there is an even more curious variant in the Greek
legend of Alcestis and Admetus. The gods were wrangling
about Admetus and finally patched the compromise that on
the day of his death he would be spared on condition that
a member of his family die voluntarily for love of him.

"This day came sooner than Admetus expected," as Robert
Graves tells us. "Admetus ran in haste to his old parents,
clasped their knees, and begged each of them in turn to sur-
render him the butt end of existence. Both roundly refused,
saying that they still derived much enjoyment from life, and
that he should be content with his appointed lot, like every-
one else."

There is a certain astringent quality to that family relationship that does cut into the sweetness of things as we have
them arranged. I don't say that I respect outright the refusal
of the merchant's two older daughters to deliver themselves

over to the beast, but I experience a good tweak of admiration for Admetus' mum and dad because they had the nerve to hold on to the butt end of their existence in the face of this impertinent request from a full-grown adult I don't care whose son he is.

I take these scattered examples of fictive family life as kinds of lien that parents have historically pressed on their children. At its core, the lien that one human being has had against the autonomy of another is psychological, I know, and only reinforced by societal institutions. In any case I am not a clinician, and I lay out this range of maternal responses that western human history knows with Clym's mother at the one end, and Admetus' at the other, and I see easily, I even condone, the doomed over-close bond between Mrs. Yeobright and her son that keeps him a kind of emotional satellite unable to leave her orbital path. Timeless is their drama that plays itself out at the edge of that bare purple-brown bitter beautiful heath where Lear walked and I have too. It would be anachronistic of me to tilt with Mrs. Yeobright, an undoubting woman in an undoubting world where an orderly hierarchical view obtained (which is an exclusionary view, be it noted, a looking after of me and mine). It is unreasonable that I should judge her harshly for the lien she pressed against the soul of her son. And I can't promise myself that Mrs. Yeobright's cry will never escape me.

At the other end of the maternal spectrum is the mother of Admetus, and I'm not sure that I won't at some time and for some reason withdraw from a blood tie in her blunt way. I can't visualize this woman very well. What I think of as a cool ancient Greek is really Roman (the farthest east I've been is Italy). A somewhat stony angular figure, toga-draped in the Hellenistic style, she is seated imperturbable, her knees jutting at angles, resting against one end of a sarcophagus, her husband at the other, a very white family tableau in the much-remarked-upon white light of Greece. As an autonomous woman she is a rather fierce sample.

I may cherish autonomy unduly, it having come to me so late. There is a *seeming* autonomy that you notice in all the campus uprisings (as well as in young black racists) manifested in the indiscriminate flailing out against authority, by the shrill, frantic abusive, dirty-name-calling, dirty-word-scrawling student—and so many of them girls. With the customary irony in human affairs, it is by these that established society knows and condemns the revolutions, while it is often these who have not so far managed to separate themselves from father or mother, but in fact all remain mutually garroted by a parental sponsorship of youthful rebellion, as I had meant to illustrate by the mothers who send up coffee and sandwiches to the beseigers of university buildings, and by that nice wine from Mme Debray.

"I have lived only for him." Mrs. Yeobright can announce this proudly, unself-consciously, in taut accord with the dour harmony of an unfrivolous world view. But it's the last thing I could permit myself to say to another human being. It shocks me. It is a statement that represents a disabling claim upon another human soul, and Clym is disabled, and finally undone.

In regard to psychological man, this mutation with a most welcome sensitivity to the uniqueness, the inviolability of each of us, I wonder whether the irony is that he seems "but slenderly to know himself," when he is father, when she is mother? Does he fare well as parent, for instance, with respect to the inviolability of his own child? He is released now from the ordering, formalizing, mitigating authority of church, state, custom, and those intrusive liens which traditional authority underwrote, so all there is left for him to beware of is the too-tight entwining of himself around the growing spirit of his offspring.

This new breed has nailed man back up at the crux, has insisted upon his ethical fiber, his humane attributes, the centrality of love in him and for him. But as father and mother perhaps they love love too well. They know about am- bivalence, allow for it intellectually, see it zigzag through their marriage, put to its account their estrangement from their own parents, but where they feel it in themselves in regard to their own children, this bad side of the good, this hate side of the love, they have to deny it, eradicate it. They won't escape these children. They can't repress them. They aren't even able to put them to bed.

Those children don't have to come up through the ranks (the way I did, the way Tony and the girls did) before they can *demand* to be seen first (and always), *demand* to be heard first (and always), living as they do in a world without rank, without time. Sometimes when I am in their houses I am nearly overcome by what their parents must endure, and heroic endurers it turns out they are. It isn't the endurance of political man waiting upon the democratic process. It is the endurance of the constant interchange with little children who are over-sensitized too early to too many nuances, an endurance reserved for psychological man whose insight into others has achieved an advanced state but whose insight into himself probably has not.

He must endure the endless presence of his children. His parenthood is predicated upon some kind of self-sacrifice that he doesn't see, the sacrifice of deep solitary silence; self-sacrifice, the contract with one signature. Nor can his children be alone, lie quiescent, retreat, rest, lapse into a dumb surface stillness while growth goes on beneath. Instead their points of sensitivity are forced to proliferate, become ever more refined, more exquisite, more dependent upon the care and cultivation of an exquisite father, a refined mother, and it is back and forth, back and forth, that the charged emotions thread from parent to child to parent, and are tightened and binding, and the end is a man with a strong lien pressed against him. I can't believe in the promise of his autonomy.

One has the impression, very generally speaking, that in earlier ages emotional imbalance was rare. It did not disable many people, nor did it alter the course of societies. That would be another unexamined assumption. Marc Bloch, in describing the natural disasters and constant acts of violence in his *Feudal Society,* says they "gave life a quality of perpetual insecurity. This was probably one of the principal reasons for the emotional instability so characteristic of the feudal era." It is also characteristic of our era, of us, the parents, and it follows, of our children, this gifted breed. How bitter to think that the failure to know oneself will be the undoing of such extraordinary promise.

XIII The Retirement of the Donor Sex

*Souls have no sexes. In the better part
they are both men.*
ROBERT BOLTON (ca. 1641)

All the revolutions are about autonomy. I remember examining, at the beginning of this personal odyssey, the possibility
that the sexual revolution might perhaps be only the women's
auxiliary of the student revolution, but I don't think so now.
I believe instead that the sexual revolution is the most elemental of all changes. It is certainly the most elemental, small
wonder, in me, since as to the others, it has been easy to shed,
given twenty whole years, my insensitivity about racial oppres-
sion, and it has been a great relief to see the young reject the
American Platitude. Wholly unanticipated and indeed startling to me was the discovery that I personally and all "unweeting" experienced the sexual revolution.

As to my own daughters, from the little ones who don't play
house to the older ones who are unkindly impatient with the
women's liberation movement, it would be hard for me to say
whether they have been the enabling force for me or I for
them. In the beginning was the word that Eve was made from
Adam's rib, and all the way through history until now she's

been on the side and diminutive, has had a sense of secondariness that I have known myself. Well, my daughters don't have it, and I have some friends among the younger women who don't have it. They've never wrestled with this subsidiary feeling as I have. They seem to have been born primary, *primae inter pares.*

When I refer to the sexual revolution, I have all along *not* meant the movement to secure women's legal and economic equality. A while ago I would have thought I had meant that myself, taking a woman's competence to be a bank director or an astronaut, the *training* of her for these roles, and bundling this terrible cleverness together with that interior female peace that the young I admire seem to have—that the word *equality* doesn't catch. Now I see that a really flourishing new woman feels an uncompeting, unbifurcated worthiness in which her female sexuality is integrated into her general capabilities (and failures) and doesn't have to be especially pled for or defended or denied. She doesn't need to cut men down.

I do not deride the liberation movement. I support it. But I'm not talking about it. I preceded it. For a long time I had been wandering lonely as a cloud in that private territory of the female self, when all at once I saw a crowd on this very territory, hosts of other women—hosts and hosts and hosts— and I couldn't have been more surprised than if they'd been golden daffodils. Emotionally, I greeted them warmly. It would be impossible for me to deny anybody the effort to find what I have so freshly come upon. Politically they radicalized me. The political arm of a political woman is tough biceptually and convincing when you feel it around your shoulders.

I am politically participatory. I gladly support any action

that causes to be unstifled a small part of a day, a small part of a life, that effects what I want to call, regardless, and non-pejoratively, an Act of Enablement—an act which is the most you can do for another human being. The people who do this, who release others from harassment, who settle for absence of pain as a political end, carry into the psychological age—and it's the essential ethical thing to do—the sense of responsible citizenship of the political animal. Is pleasure the absence of pain? It has never seemed a joyful enough definition to me. But as passenger on the Long Island Railroad I would settle for it. As citizen. As a woman delivered from the unfair treatment accorded by law and custom to my sex, I would settle for it.

But the pleasure of this *interior* integration that marks *for me* the sexual revolution seems more joyful than the flat landscape the absence of pain summons to mind. For me the revolution hasn't been a political gain, an improved social condition, but a psychological perspective, a healthy thrust towards truth for woman and therefore for man. I only see this lately. A couple of years ago I set up Ibsen's Nora as a foil against my stern view of what you did when you suddenly gained new insight, suddenly matured. You become *more responsible*. But Nora walked out on her husband and little children, abandoned her responsibilities; and I pinioned her. I couldn't imagine. I failed to imagine, what had really happened to her. The closest I came was what I would call for the moment a political truth, since I saw the externals, of course: that she had been kept, by society's design, a sweet, beguiling, delightful child (what to my dismay our children aren't encouraged to be even when they're children), her mind bound like the feet of little mandarin girls so that she would remain permanently dependent and stumble charmingly through life. Then the sky falls down and she sees that her nature has never been her own possession, hers to *become* with, to make life what she will with. I never begrudged her her indignation, but I thought that the mature thing to do once she'd cooled down was to go back into that doll's house and reorder it on grown-up lines. But she walked out for good. Suppose everybody just walked out!

I saw in her a woman who moved from childhood to adolescence, that's all. I thought the issue was maturity and that if she'd really grown up she would not only put things in shape around the house, but trot out to organize a women's suffrage local. I failed entirely to see how close she had come to being nobody, to being left with only the vestiges of character, that "her responsibilities" lost their meaning with the child-self that contracted them, that she must have felt frighteningly light-weight, having been so cleaned of meaning, a germinal self under the single necessity to start at once and at an alarmingly late date to grow into a person. If that was what it was, then I agree she had no other obligations. She would not have been able to go back to her husband under a contract to which her post-traumatic self could not possibly have been signatory.

To talk about contracts. *Lien* is a contractual word. The presumptive right of the self-sacrificing mother to a fair return on her dedication deals with the legal exchanges of natural law. Mrs. Yeobright could call on all humanity to witness that her position was unimpeachable. And I've felt it necessary to worry about the unconscious contract the new breed makes with its young, fearing the most admirable woman may involve herself too intimately and too unremittingly in the growth of her own child, making her a self-sacrificing parent, however unintended, and obligating the child by too heavy a gift.

On the other hand, I feel that there are so many new givens in the situation that this may not be the determining factor in the question of whether or not an autonomous human being is in the making. A prominent given is this: while there may be still, however disguised, a contractual basis to the relationship between mother and child as ancient as the realm of the traditionary king of Wessex, the historical contract that *bound* wife to husband, *bound* woman to man, has been abruptly canceled. It is *en train* now in marriage that there is either a mutuality, a shared consent to the division of labor, or there's an end to the relationship, an end to the honoring of it. Mutuality is the ethical base. Whatever is still contractual about marriage doesn't rest any more on sexual rank. For the point worth making here, I think, is that the egalitarian, the leveling factor that is a primary attribute of all these revolutions and rather steam-rolls over established rank and color and age and every boundary line including geographical, has certainly flattened the hierarchical relationship in marriage. Man and woman enter one to one into their association, and may leave it one from one, and their inherent sense of parity is as much a part of the psychological truth for a new man as for a new woman.

This is poetic, I know. It is more the flag they sail under than a description of some large group of extra-wise, extra-free mutations who are about to effect an extra-ordinary union. But *our* flag under which a woman has been sent unquestioning to find the whole meaning of her life in the single institution of marriage (but a man is never expected to find his whole meaning in it) has been fluttering ever more feebly as the century unrolls. The *idea* of woman's equality, finally full-sprung about the time Nora marched out the door, has had to seep slowly through a few generations before it burrowed into the soul to become this sense of inner worthiness, as though there had to be a breathing spell until a woman could cope with the entitlement to full humanity. It is an idea that arises in Victorian society and then, 1914—Forever, the American women, those who were not ground down by life, were left to drift in a hiatus between the statement of equality and the feeling of it, and they were badly under-used. It is the line of under-used women which interests me, as it is my line, and I know it well. I regarded marriage as a total solution while avowing otherwise. I made everything I could of being a commendable wife and mother, and it was a partial story. The greater part of myself, the greater part of my life, I must take care of.

"What do you make of the fact," my friend Brett asked me last night, "that the students arriving at Smith and Princeton in the last few years are the first parent-reared children?" What do I make of it? Well, first I think many depressed parents would get more depressed by this sociological thought, and perhaps it would be a kindness not to mention it. But that is flippant, and I flip it the other way. These children, very early and in great numbers, got too much *first-quality* attention, and they've grown up with an ethical certainty, an ethical centricity, that they won't be jollied out of. That reflects well upon us, and it is the thesis of this book that we did transmit the finest values of Western civilization very well, but we didn't take serious advantage of them ourselves. It is as though we were only carriers.

Carriers, under-used women, who are we? I once read in an unsigned review in the *Times Literary Supplement* the uncredited remark by a Scots psychoanalyst that "American women receive too much *poor quality* attention," the least subtle model of us being, surely, the blue-haired Mother's Day matron. The problem has been throughout the century that my line of urban middle-class woman has been underused, and while it is something to ponder, that our (middle-class) generation is the first to rear our own children because of the arrival of household machinery and the departure of domestic servants, we were not the first to have too much time on our hands, nor to be encouraged to make frivolous use of it: to make a lifework of Getting Dressed and Going Shopping and showing up at the PTA. Though anointed equal, we were expected to find the meaning of our lives in marriage, and destined to be disappointed, and make culprits of our husbands. I know that in my mother's generation it was a deeply entrenched middle-class thought that a man with pride wouldn't let his wife work. My father thought that, I remember his telling me. In his social economy it seemed a fair bargain that a man would support their life and a woman would grace it, but later he thought it wasn't fair. The evolving consciousness of one sex will cause the other to evolve too.

It is taking perhaps a hundred years for a revolution so fundamental to have occurred in the minds of women, and the condition of the American marriage may after all improve as a consequence. I do not think the passing of the old belief that a woman's meaning is bracketed by marriage is to be regretted. I know lots of women who have shriveled mind and soul, and not many who have flourished in marriage. They are hard to live with.

I know how it happens. You don't start hard. You look to your husband when your children come, for your adult relief, for all your comfort, amusement, intellectual stimulation, and obscurely, for your justification. And he fails you. There are two styles of revenge for this, to bang or to whimper, and I think that I would have taken the second and worse. That is to say, I think my natural rhythm would not be hospitable to the cycle of rage and abatement that would have me periodically burst into abuse and list the unfeeling things Paul has said and done to me since June 1949. I take more naturally to being Hurt but Brave, and more helpless is the man whose self is gnawed and nibbled at by the steady, unfluctuating, and *unappeasable* force, not of fury, but of frailty. Unbelievable is the weight of this frailty. It is a style of resentment that inches along towards total possession of the personality and lets you rather generously not confine the source of pain to the one man whom by odd coincidence you happened to marry, but has you very sensitive to wrongs from wherever and whomever, but you forgive them, but you suffer. This is when I might have thought that there but for the grace of God go I.

I did *not* think about God's grace in this matter when we were driving through rural Sicily last winter and passed slowly by the bleak squares of the poorest little towns and I saw hard-used, lean, lined, shrunken black-shawled women of my age who looked seventy, but I thought of it during Christmas week in our beautiful hotel in Taormina when I saw hard and soft, medium-rich women of my age at the full flush of an empty life of hair-dressing and clothes-changing and mink-stoling, under-used, terribly under-used. There go I, I thought, but for the luck that dogs my life.

But not there go our girls.

The last significant imposed limitation of freedom for our daughters in marriage will not be economic or biologic but geographic. If he is in Arabic Studies at Princeton, she would not accept her psychiatric residency in San Francisco, I hope. Is that unequal? It's why I bicker with the word. Mutuality, the provision for the self-esteem for the two dissimilar but complimentary sexes in our species, contains for me the shared acceptance of male priority in certain things and of female in others.

O tempora! O mores! I am skirting the outsides of the subject of today's sexual attitudes, but it would be presumptuous to imagine my way inside a girl of eighteen or twenty, and I'm not willing to report too intimately from inside forty to forty-five. I bring up *tempora* for temporality, that other primary attribute of the revolutionary position, the changed relationship to time, the singular concern with the nowness of one's actions and judgments, which has a lot more to do with the relaxed sexuality than the pill has. Relaxed sexuality, relaxed everything, our children are dropping in and out of school, work, love, family, countries, "relationships," and even on this end of Harrison Avenue there are moments when a grizzled parent overcomes his enlightenment—the Puritan Ethic being

the Financial Angel of the local revolutionaries, after all—
and puts an old question to his boy: "What are you going to
be? A bum all your life!" That for *O tempora,* and for *O mores,*
a long shuddering *Oh* for their mores.

The new temporality tampers quite mischievously with the
old marriage contract. The great consternation written into
those letters to me about it's being God's will that a woman
preserve her body as a special gift for her husband was a
warning not to fool around with that contract. What those
women saw (but I didn't see it) was that I had devalued sex
as currency in the social market, had said by implication that
it wasn't going to underwrite our traditional relationships very
forcefully any longer. They have a great stake in the soundness of this currency, for as it is unambiguous to be the
donor, to be *defined* for life, so it is the peak of maternal relief to hear their daughters party to the sentence. "I now pronounce you man and wife." What a sweet sound, really, sweet
as the chopping of the cleaver, because is there a greater desire than to want to know one's children are permanently
safe, permanently settled, that weddings are not whimsical
affairs, a human convention, but a divine commandment?

If you are comfortable with being the Donor Sex, the willing giver of yourself because you are lesser, because a woman's role is biologically assigned by God and Nature, then it's
impossible to believe that the world would not come to an
end if young girls began to depart from the script, ad lib, take
an exploratory ramble outside onto terrain they thought was
as morally neuter as the moon, and just even—*horrible dictu*
—walk right out of the whole framework of received truth.
How these revolutions have sent in disarray all the orderly

battalions of received truth! What they have done to that jigsaw puzzle—not one piece, but every piece chewed on and
mangled. And I know what they fear. *I* saw it, in my childhood, that flash of a question with a touch of panic in it:
suppose they just walk out? These women writing sternly to
me could have seen it in *The Graduate*. At the end of the
movie (a kind of dopey) Benjamin storms the church where
his (kind of dopey) girl is getting married to Another, and
he arrives in the nick of time to hear that final, irreversible,
divine pronouncement that she is forever somebody else's
wife, *and then* he scoops her off to be nonetheless his own for
those fifty years I wonder what they're going to do in. This
is not *our* nick of time, goodness knows.

What is called morality does seem to have focused rather
narrowly upon the rules about woman's sexuality, that her
life range was a simple and unadventurous swing from virginity to fidelity which, being her God-given preference, has
served marriage and the family as solidly as the Gold Standard has served world trade. There is a great problem about
the Gold Standard today, since it doesn't work. It is too simple, too naïve because, of all things, it turns out that international finance is psychologically complex too. Curious that
there were two questions I asked as a child that never brought
a clear answer, and the one was (after the facts-of-life talk),
"But how does your body know that you are married so that
it can make a baby out of that egg?" and the other was, "Why
does everybody agree that gold is the most valuable?" because
I, as a matter of fact, happened to think silver was prettier.
And now everybody doesn't agree. The young don't agree,
and they won't negotiate their contracts with each other on

this ancient coin of the realm. They treat female sexuality, virginity and monogamy as if it were all wampum, all glass beads and paper flowers, all pleasure; they fasten their love with love buttons.

Now it is true that they've walked out on the solemnity of sex, dropped the moral gold standard, without fears, regrets, without a thought simply vacated that vast concept. We can wait for them to be struck down, wait for them to be sorry, but I believe we wait in vain. From the dark porch of this abandoned concept we watch them gamboling wanton in the golden meadow, but it is probably once again merely *our* perverse obsession with proscribed sexual behavior that makes us see nothing but promiscuity and nakedness, a regular orgy of immorality, while actually it would be better to look at what is now moral *horizontally,* so to speak, to see that making love hasn't been elevated and it hasn't been demoted, but it has been rolled over to leave room for other absorbing needs like letting live, instead of killing, and valuing people instead of things.

I thought the world would come to an end if they just walked out, but that golden meadow where the love pennants fly is all affirmation. "They have no shame! They have no modesty! They are immoral!" we gasp, looking out through jaded eyes from the dark porch. But virginity as a test of morality has been discredited for a long time. Certainly I never tested my morality by it when I was at Smith, not mine nor anybody else's. I had shame. I had modesty of the nervous skirt-pulling variety. A bunch of Amazons we were, wrapped in layers of clothing, in ever-present peril of suddenly having a wrong piece of us show naked to the eye, so that when the

short skirts of the wartime economy gave way to the volu-
minous wrappings of the New Look and let you wonderfully
expand and flop, many modesty muscles must have atrophied,
with no sign, of course, that they have since been impressed
back into use on account of the mini situation.

I feel a true regret for the passing of modesty. Really, I
have done what I could to engage our daughters to consider
its aesthetic properties. The woman who kept our house when
I was a child and taught me my manners believed that one of
the most important things in life was to wear underclothes
that were in good condition because you never knew when
you might be in an accident and brought to the hospital,
where it would be discovered that your underwear was torn,
but not by the truck that ran over you. I've taken this obliga-
tion to heart for life, although thank goodness it has never
had to pass the Emergency Room test, and I have passed it
on to our children. And what could have come in handier,
now that they don't feel that nice shame any more. Sexually,
they are no longer under wraps.

They have no shame and they have no modesty, but they
seem to me actually more moral than we were, their morality
more reasonable, less tormented. It's easy for them. They are
invited to espouse, and do espouse our ancient ethical scheme
rid of many redundant taboos. They will make love and not
war. On good days I think the condition of their ethics is
superb, and it's their ethics and not the sight of their under-
pants, really, that must be the measure of their worth, and I
would be willing to match their purity and goodness against
St. Ursula and her eleven thousand virgins, about whom I always retained some scepticism.

XIV In Hoc Signe

Al Capp's in London for a holiday. He's still a liberal, he says, but the liberal establishment has gone arrogant, remote, and Fascist. "I hate puberty worshippers. These people who worship the ill-educated, the insolvent, the helpless and graceless as fountains of wisdom." Young people, he thinks, should be "helped, sheltered, ignored, clubbed if necessary. I'm a great admirer of Mayor Daley."

The Manchester Guardian Weekly

Yes, well, Mr. Capp, I myself began this thesis as the liberal who stood aghast before Their Scene, how unlovely it was and unhygienic; and how unmeasured were Their Things. But I never have become so arrogant, remote, and Fascist (a wide swing with words, Mr. Capp; you have become your own Nogoodnik), however much I am wooed and won by the young, as to be ready to divorce myself from Western civilization. I'm in love with Western civilization; I am sworn to its Printed Word. But your message to the English people reminds me of the need to be orderly and proportionate as becomes this dear heritage, so I had better separate what in the young I appear to be "worshipping" from what I deplore, marking in the middle a lot of things I merely notice while remaining detached in a becoming way. In the end perhaps I could take this very word *proportion* and send it across with a message of peace to the other side of thirty.

I think you can be against napalm *and* littering. It was two years ago that Julie and Maggie led me to the record player and made me listen to the autobiographical ballad of Arlo Guthrie which begins with his dumping Alice's garbage on private property, and winds up at the induction center where the U.S. Army is wondering about his character. "You gotta lot of damn gall to ask me if I rehabilitated myself. You wanna know if I'm moral enough to burn kids, houses, and villages after being a litterbug?" I listened to it twice (but I haven't seen the movie) and I thought that record was "tough," once our children's highest word of praise, but I use it with both meanings, ours and theirs. Since then littering and napalm have become a symbolic device for me to represent the polarization of generations and generational values. I can trace a physical feeling of despair like the wriggle of an eel down my gullet, over a news photograph in the *Times* of the faces of Vietnam children who are caught watching their mother being "interrogated"—not a remarkable reaction. But when I'm driving down Elm Street or along a throughway and suddenly my attention is attracted by the swift furious flutter of some light bit of trash tossed out from the car ahead, there in a split second is that same despair in my throat; a disproportionate reaction.

Do all these pieces have to interlock, so that to be moral is to be clean, modest, ashamed, to be philosophical and know how to endure, to vow the pledge of common friendship *and* common hate? And if there is a new ethic that has broken through the framework of the old one and is rich, disorderly, contradictory, what are we all going to do with it anyhow, what are Benjamin and his girl going to do with their fifty years, and what indeed is any of us going to do with the rest of his allotted time?

("I am no prophet and here's no great matter.")

I am no prophet, but I presume to guess about Benjamin, that he's basically a beaten guy and will make his money in plastics after all. In the end he is his father's son and his wonderment and hurt will be soothable by a sort of Rotarian Guru, modern but moderate, more or less in the way his father might draw comfort from Billy Graham. Billy Graham is modern but moderate. Time after time a man will come to him and say, "Billy, I'm rich, I'm successful, my name has been in lights on every theater marquee in Europe and America, (*or* "I own oil wells on three continents," *or* "I'm the biggest man in plastics") but Billy, I'm not happy." That's Benjamin. He was not happy.

But Benjamin, as I have thought from the very beginning, doesn't really represent himself *in toto* to the young as singularly admirable and imitable. He represents himself as *victim*. What he is saying is there is a toxic quality to parts of our culture which produces stupor, coma, and convulsions, symptoms Webster's ascribes to "narcotic in poisonous doses," and which the young ascribe to the drugging effects of living in *our* scene, the Establishment Scene, what the black GIs call the Giant PX. Among the complex ranging variations of this new breed Benjamin stands (in my eyes) for defeat. In the beginning I wondered why our own great big healthy lot of children thought *The Graduate* was so fine, and now I think it is because they feel the poignancy of failure in these worst cases. I don't expect them to agree that this is what they feel, of course.

However, taking Benjamin as one, and also as representative of his kind, and including Hippies, and taking Tony and our daughters and the Smith girls, the boys at UMass, Princeton, Williams, Amherst, and the members of the Northampton High School band, and an assortment of the younger faculty, taking them all in their tremendous variety and individuality, multiplied across the continent, I make them the composite of the new breed, good and ill. But I understand that this view is elitist, that I am dealing only with, broadly speaking, my own middle-class kind. (I am no prophet and no sociologist either.) Now I set them all out over a vast open field to examine what they add up to, many thousands of them, hundreds of thousands of them, two hundred, three hundred thousand of them, with their long hair, combed and uncombed, their beads, their dirty, clean, ugly, pretty clothes, or their nakedness, their deliberately provocative sexuality (deliberately provocative, that is, to their elders), their folk rock with the peace themes and the love themes, and their grass (grass on the grass alas). By these signs shall ye know them.

And I take a reluctant drag on drugs for I am deeply unqualified to be openminded about even marijuana. I hate the drugs. But I have to note for my own sake that three springs ago an authority on drugs from the state of New York talked to the students at Smith very convincingly, and I remember his making the point that whatever else marijuana was, it wasn't the American way out, our crutch, our outlet. Our crutches were alcohol and tobacco and incalculable cultural change would result in our taking on somebody else's native bad habit. Well, like it or not, for our young this isn't true any more. It's their habit, and those three hundred thousand people sharing that yellow meadow are also sharing pot illegally, at least most of them, if only for the occasion. Barefoot, tangled hair, soiled and mussed, whatever they are wearing if they are wearing anything, they are so packed into that meadow for my examination, in groups, clusters, haphazard rows, in no order and only disorder, that what comes to my mind is the picture of the beach at Coney Island from a heat wave in my childhood, of overlapping naked arms and legs and torsos. Not beautiful either, those bygone people, if you see them painted by Paul Cadmus with contempt for the human comedy. They have escaped the hot pavements and their hot boxed lives for the day and are drinking beer and leaving rubbish. Two happy crowds, pleasure seeking, pleasure finding, from two different worlds.

A couple of hundred thousand people make a very large crowd. Sheer numbers have changed the meaning of the idea of crowds. There is no question but that the Western mind has not been able to encompass the consequence to human life of our plummeting death rate, although this century attests to the unbearability of it: the word *liebensraum* leads to the word *Auschwitz*. But it's not always unbearable, and in fact there is evidence that man can adapt to what would seem to me an abrasive intimacy. I need solitude, but I need fellowship. But I need solitude more, and the needle pointing to my emotional pressures rarely wobbles off to the right where the crowds are. I read about Essenes or Owenites or

Hippie Communes with sympathy but never wistfully. It may be because this house, being home to seven people, passes well enough for a commune and cultivates wonderfully a taste for being alone. At seven-forty in the morning, when I've kissed the last child and watch her for a moment troop off down the street to school, and I turn back down our big winter-dark hall where I feel the emptiness of this large house resound, I'm a happy woman. Some time during the afternoon, though, I begin waiting and listening. But basically you could say my communal needs have been more than satisfied, and I have to brace myself to regard benignly the attractiveness of crowds. I can't imagine heading myself towards that meadow, onto that beach, without a gun stuck in my ribs.

Nevertheless, the line is very thin between the contradictions we contain, and depending on the crowd's touch, we will thrill or shriek, "the touch," as Mill observes about something else, "which determines whether a stone, set in motion at the top of an eminence, shall roll down one side or on the other." And I note there's only a suffix-worth of difference between the deep-meaning phrases Human Bond and Human Bondage. One is certainly entitled to be cynical about the bond, but the accumulated acid cynicism of history has not eaten it away. It links, this bond, the fact that, concomitant with the frightening dimensions of our population problem, grows the capacity to amass ourselves willingly and even joyfully for apolitical reasons in giant sprawls, or on the other hand to converge longitudinally, so to speak, for political reasons, as with Gandhi's march to the sea, or our black march on Washington, or the March against Death.

Numbers, hundreds of thousands, millions of people, each by his private decision voluntarily combines himself, gladly prepared to be accumulated in such conditions of density that I would have supposed to be intolerable, and with this amassing to make a *statement,* by deliberation or by indeliberation.

In examining the very likely rebuttal that there's nothing all that new in the young that warrants their being elevated to something so portentous as a finer mutation of human being, and whether the present revolutionary situation isn't a swollen crest of a recurrent wave of generational protest, history being full of a rich assortment of parallels, I must register my conviction that our vast twentieth-century *numbers* of people, no matter what they are doing (or having done to them), make a qualitative change in the doing of it. Omitting the ways that a worldwide communications system, and television in particular, queen of communications, distorts meaning, multiplies numbers, accelerates change, there are still three hundred thousand on the meadow this year, a million and a half someplace else next year, and incalculable numbers ready to hear and assent. The numbers are a new given. But regardless of the numbers, on the beach at Coney Island, and on the march through India, and on the march through Washington, except in the minds of a scattered few, there were no revolutions already accomplished. Revolutions which define an irreversible change of viewpoint were being initiated, stimulated, coaxed, prodded by the marches, while the white Coney Island crowd was pre-revolutionary then, as a white Coney Island crowd probably still is. Among those who join together on the meadow, however, significant fundamental changes in outlook have already taken place. What this generation of that meadow has in common with those bodies on the seashore of my childhood is a wonderful time. Everybody has a wonderful time, then and now, and that's the end of the similarity. The rest is contrast.

The wonderful times themselves are produced by contrast because in the one instance you took children, picnic, grandma, grandpa, auntie, subway to escape a hard marginal existence, and the whole of pre-war American society is represented on that beach if you know how to read the evidence. (Like the interpretation of dreams: if I understand the meaning of what Freud is said to have thought about a man's dream, if you knew how to explore and read one dream you would know the whole man. It would be his statement.) At Coney Island on a Sunday summer afternoon it's the white American Dream surfacing for the moment, but the massive dark rest of it is there beneath.

But spread over that golden meadow thirty years later is one generation and one class, roughly speaking, cutting out from the white American Dream, fleeing swimming pools, private beach clubs, relaxed, roomy, expensive summer retreats, all the most desirable things. Not desired. And there aren't many blacks in this particular field. The blacks are waiting out our children. They say our sons and daughters have no soul and they had better go and get some soul and then, and *then* maybe they'll talk about being brothers. You have to see this meadow as filled with soul-searchers. The Coney Island trippers, voting a third term for FDR, still believed that Progress did the marching, and they waited upon it.

And unique, unprecedented, and unrepeatable as is each of these young, they are all gathered on the meadow by a process of self-selection, and they share in the mass (but they aren't the mass) these attributes I have been trying to make real to our past-conditioned senses: an egalitarianism and a telescoped temporality. Sun-baked, soaked, bitten, hungry, still—incredibly—they aren't frayed by the too-close contact, the touching. It is the opposite. They touch to feel their fellowship, to enter the common friendship. They come together and find the joy in that communal love the rest of us have known only under siege, London love during the London blitz: but of course they do feel themselves under the siege of *our* dead reckoning.

Still it is hard to guess whether the drugs are to be congratulated for maintaining a benevolent high, the drugs instead of the people. How would that enormous communal bash fare on alcohol? Bash would be the word. Is it their luck or their wisdom or their tragedy to combine a recognition of greater ethical injunctions with the chemistry that disjoins them from acting? After they've put in a good working day expressing their supreme contempt for us, whipped themselves into a proper fury, why, they go out through their outlet to defuse themselves with pot or hash in their communal way, calmly disconnecting themselves from caring. And they've left us, meanwhile, in a raging hurt, in a passion of defensiveness, fearfully charged up by this indictment leveled by our own children, needing a double martini, two double martinis. "To superminds with love," they write to the world's eminent scientists gathered in Stockholm, "We do not trust you and we are not grateful."

Drugs lie like an incubus over their fine promise. Does one know when a life marked by occasional defusing becomes a life marked by diffusion? In a generation where age and rank count very little and the seeking of this fellowship of protest-cum-pot has skidded down from eighteen to sixteen to fourteen, isn't it a nightmare thought that these most sensitive young, their generation's deepest carers, may be putting themselves out of commission for good? Will the drugs in the end neutralize the moral energy and insight of this whole new breed, will they be in that field like the lilies, neither toiling nor spinning?

There is another field in the American story, the field of poppies that Dorothy had to cross on her way to the Wizard of Oz, but nothing living could get through without growing so groggy with intoxication that it must drop to sleep forever. And from there to the poppies of Flanders Field and an association I make with the mindless slaughter in the trenches of the First World War, where the flower (flower) of English manhood and the flower of French manhood are killed and so the remainder, the stalks, had to assume the leadership of the Western world after 1918. Alas. And I've thought if the strongest part of this new breed is under-mined, cut off from the numerical support of those who are disabled by drugs or depression, then the leadership will fall to people of limited imagination, people very like us. To think that way lies madness.

Uncomfortable as I am with the subject of the displacement of alcohol by drugs, I recognize this much, that in a generation for whom the value of time has condensed to the present, who are non-hierarchical, not exclusionary or terri-

torial or violent, the turning to drugs is not ironic or antithetical to the underlying permissive spirit. If we have
previously been a violent people we have also been a whiskey-
drinking people. But this new breed is not violent, and their
outlet isn't needed for the release of pent-up violence, I don't
think. Indeed it seems to me the most distinguishing attribute
of the political, sexual and, even black revolutions (this is
wish being father to the thought) is pacifism. I have hedged
towards this from the first pages, not knowing what to do with
the aggressive instincts, not knowing how these young can
have sloughed them off. There is a story about Freud and
Einstein, that with the advent of Hitler, Einstein wrote in
anguish to Freud and said that as they both could see war
coming, wasn't there something they could do to prevent it?
And Freud is said to have answered, Nothing, that war is the
consequence of man's aggressive energy, but that they, these
two men, were perhaps examples of a pacific mutation of
the human race, small in numbers, lonely, and destined to
perish. Whether this is apocryphal or misrepresented I don't
know, but aggressive energy, insofar as I understand it to
contain the *necessity* to kill one's own kind, is something I
don't recognize in myself, or readily detect in many people
I know, and in fact in my school days, with a little encourage-
ment, lots of us could have declared ourselves pacific mutations and given those remote and august geniuses some company.

The pacifism in these young is entirely credible to me, intellectually and emotionally as consonant with the expanding
sensitivity of the psychological age, although I don't regard
it as an ideology, pledged and vowed, but only as a point of

view ever liable to be shaken. And this is logical enough, for the leveling that sends you bounding across boundaries makes you an internationalist, makes you not so territorial in your orientation, not forever needing to defend your borders. That these young are Freud's pacific mutation surviving because of fitness, indeed unexpectedly multiplying, is a happy evolutionary surprise that shouldn't pass without thanks in case it is ephemeral.

And I even wonder about this best of the triad of attributes, pacifism, this heightened revulsion against killing your own kind, whether it doesn't derive from that most elemental of all revolutionary changes, the change in woman. When I look for the words to identify the traditional woman, a Mrs. Yeobright, the meaning of whose life is confined exclusively to her household, I see that I need to say *exclusive* to make my point, and then I see *exclude* in that. She was a very territorial creature. She drew a circle, brought her own inside, and the rest was alien, and the circle was a wall. Now that's not what our young woman does. There's no wall. She sketches a circle, and it still indicates the centrality of her position as a member of the family, but she moves easily back and forth across it, no customs at the border, and can go round the world and back again as a member of humanity. She includes. Why, even I included.

Now as to the young, in looking the field over, I can't really say that in pacifism, egalitarianism, this generally enlarged and deeper commitment to humanist values, in *these* signs, ye shall know them right off the bat. Mr. Capp doesn't see these signs at all, and he's not alone, and I have no doubt, were I to plead a little before him he would regard me stonily and say, "it is your figment, Mrs. Seton, your figment and I don't give a fig for it!"

What we see in the way of outward signs would not lead us to surmise the least intimation of inner grace, not the least. But to some extent it is our eye that is at fault, our early *reductio ad absurdum* training. Cavalierly we take the whole spectrum from hippies to the Maoist faction of SDS, which embraces really just about as wide a spread of attitudes, tastes, and personalities as can humanly exist, and we reduce them to one particularly haughty, nasty, dirty prototype which we call the Younger Generation. Then we find their appearance, their manners, their arrogance unbearable. And haven't we made every effort to approach them and they Just Walk Out in the middle of our Reason? And there is this hair fetish; it is by that sign that we know them. But is it our fetish or their fetish? And thirty years ago would we have looked at Gandhi and seen only a loincloth, been appalled, indignant, contemptuous of that loincloth?

XV   On Uncivil Discord

And I have known the eyes already, known them all—
The eyes that fix you in a formulated phrase,
And when I am formulated, sprawling on a pin,
When I am pinned and wriggling on the wall,
Then how should I begin
To spit out all the butt-ends of my days and ways?
*   And how should I presume?*

*   The Love Song of J. Alfred Prufrock*

In the course of human development the late adolescent is particularly prone to moral righteousness. More remarkable probably is how morally righteous are people over thirty, even though they haven't got this proneness. Still there is no mistaking the trait in our young and a grievous incivility in their approach to our antidisestablishmentarianism, the longest word in the English language of my childhood that I have never previously found an occasion to use. What to do about this incivility, and how serious is it? Well, very soberly, I think it can be mortally serious.

I attest to the presence these pacific mutants flourishing in America and to the expansive humanism therein and the marvelous leveling that their minds accomplish, all the while disregarding, they and I together, the one class of people, and that the largest, for whom they have no charity: the great white middle, the great white whale. The white middle class has reduced the young to a horrible stereotype, and they have returned the compliment. All of us being deadly serious, deadly. Anybody else who is across any line, is any other color, the vast varied conglomerations of Others, is glorified by this new tribe because he is other, has its respect because he is an individual.

There are three blocks in the Bronx, it says in the *Times,* that are entirely the territory of junkies and outside society, where there's not even a word of law, not even an act of order, and where between one and two out of every twenty people dies a natural death. This is not youth's drug culture, nor our drugging culture. This is straight drug and no culture at all, but only non-life, only stabbing, stealing, beating, killing, and selling the self for drugs. Eighteen or nineteen people out of every twenty on these three blocks die in the pursuit of the next dose, directly or indirectly. The young read in this a terrible indictment of a smug society guilty of criminal indifference, and that is somewhat the way I read it too. A failure of our imagination, I would put it. And they will see these eighteen or nineteen people as victims of our callous and blind piety. But for the one or two people who die of natural causes —not addicts, not running the drug maze, only terrified and preyed upon by them—for these victims of the victims of society there is little sympathy. The young have a tremendous pool of sympathy, charity, caring, but it is not inexhaustible, and by the time the victims of the victims need it there isn't any left. And that is what the great white middle largely has become, the victims of the victims.

The breach between generations has the characteristics of a class breach in which the young have declassified themselves.

Their easy latitudinarian temperament extends so laudably, so widely to the *déclassés,* to all the have-nots, led by themselves the don't-want-its, but ends abruptly at the edge of the oceanic bourgeoisie, we under water where I had us once before, they, the new land creatures, hardly dry, disdaining so much as to wet their toes. This mutation which walks upright in the sun, a friend to all its kind, in whom the aggressive energies have so waned as to be an unaccountable phenomenon, when turned towards us can become crude, nasty, vulgar, a scrawler of dirty words, a shoving, poking, bashing, violent species, painfully familiar. This peaceful mutation, this ugly revolutionary, both. And with forces, energies, impulses, traits, characteristics, knocking together in fierce contradiction to produce the very heat that sends the revolution around.

> "This utterly pacific, benevolent, loving character of the Revolution seems today a paradox—so unknown is its origin, so misunderstood its nature, and so obscured its tradition, in so short a time. The violent, terrible efforts it is obliged to make in order not to perish in a struggle with the conspiring world, have been mistaken for the Revolution itself by a forgetful generation."

I quote this against myself, taking it from an essay on Romanticism in which the author says it is really no longer possible to doubt that we are in the middle of a romantic revival. The above is from an unidentified source written before 1850. This is the stuff sent out to puncture theories like mine. That my metaphor of a pacific mutation must contain the paradox of fostering vulgarity, violence, insufferable righteousness would be all right if such an exact description of our unparalleled revolutionary condition weren't written more than a hundred years ago. Was it a strong contraction in the giving birth to a more successful breed, and is this perhaps another strong contraction? I know that there are tides in the affairs of men and that we are living in a spring tide, those coming to maturity in the fifties in a neap, that the basin of Western civilization holds a vast and increasing reservoir (to pursue another watery allusion) of those altruistic instincts about which George Eliot remarks, and from which men of timeless insight have emerged throughout history to join E. M. Forster's aristocracy. The young have just walked out before, alienated, disgusted, the American young being expatriate in Germany and then in Paris, London, Rome, and under that white light of Greece. Young men have departed from foreign policy before, to form the Abraham Lincoln Brigade, for instance, and young women have thumbed their noses at propriety, cut their hair short and flapped and shocked: all this in recent memory.

But not all this, knowing what is known now. Is it really all my figment? Have I looked at our children, clutched my throat, shriveled at their outward signs, and developed a thesis to rescue me from despair, enhancing it with flourishes microbiological, socio-anthropological, pseudo-technotronic, and politically scientific, much in the way Sullivan enhanced Gilbert? But as to technotronic I would just like to remind those people a bit too ready to lie down and be flattened by the dehumanization processes guaranteed by observers of the disciplines of technology, electronics, and bureaucracy, that the events of this past decade, which for unpredictability alone can never before in the history of mankind have been matched, these events have been excruciatingly *human*. Ponder it.

I ponder these excruciatingly human events mostly from my front porch, exhilarated or depressed, as I have noted, and I share the rue of my neighbors for the fall from grace of grace. From here, it seems, unparalleled numbers younger than thirty repudiate the establishment, the power structure, our scene, and unparalleled numbers over thirty whose scene it is, who are the establishment, the power structure, appear dismayed to be holding it all in place. But it is hard to recognize in the violent contempt they have for us an invitation to contribute a regiment or two, much less assume command. We at our age are tempered by Western civilization and by the years we've lived through; are hierarchical, do respect rank, feel ourselves custodians of the future—all subduing, disqualifying habits of mind: we're 4F in the revolutions.

And what revolting revolutionaries they can make, with their bursting into tantrums, letting themselves be led to violence by the hysterical and fanatical among them, with their slashing, smearing, their paroxysms of loathing; all of which I have intended to cover in a seemly way by the word *incivility*. And what has it all produced? I mean besides the reexamination of our foreign policy, the awakening to the actuality of our racism, the restructuring of our universities, and so on? Can it be that we are simply another blind forgetful generation that takes the violence, the incivility, for the revolutions themselves, people who would have looked at Gandhi and seen only the loincloth?

Still, I hate the incivility in itself and because it diminishes that finer, vaster ethical comprehension that I (driven desperate?) attribute to this improvement in the species. It is a backwards step. Oh but, good grief, backwards! I, a New Deal child born too soon, am too old to bear backwards with equanimity. It plunges me forward to that promised progress that was my birthright, and I seek solace, proof I'm all right, in the printed word, and I find it these last few days in the combining in my mind of something I read in J. H. Plumb's *England in the Eighteenth Century* with something of Erik Erikson's in *Gandhi's Truth.* (This is of course for home use. I am no prophet, no sociologist, no historian, and no psychoanalyst.) It has to do with progress, the rehabilitating of it. After all, I don't believe that there is nothing new under the sun, that it's *plus ça change,* that the generational struggle today is what generational struggles have always been, a game of cat's cradle. So I am naturally thrown back upon the mercy of progress.

The modern idea of progress which emerges, as I understand it, with Protestantism and the marching of the saints through this world right on into the next, and which resurges, laicized, in the eighteenth century with the belief in the perfectability of man and in it being our manifest destiny, our Anglo-American destiny, *manifestly,* to lead the way—well, I can take that idea of progress and mock and deride it with the best of them. But if I take the idea of progress, disconnected from predestination, and apply it selectively to the mechanical ingenuity of Western man and to his scientific comprehension, it seems in our timespan, so far, sustained. And if I take it further and apply it to the sophistication of the ethical sense, the extension of the covenant of caring, outward from the self, beyond family, groups, nations, beyond what Erikson calls the pseudo-species, to the human species, I think there can be traced the progress of a truth whose time has come: whether or not it has come in time.

This is an ethical question. I look up *ethics,* and Webster's gives as its meaning, "(2) the science of moral duty," and it seems to me a most moving definition (that dictionary really touches me) and rallies my whole self to the homeliness of what is right and wrong, the guiding of little children through that maze of the meanings of life by marking their progress with calibrated duties. (And I wonder if the Fourth International will have "Duty: *obs.*"). Well, if it is acceptable to apply the word *progress,* circumspectly, to physical science, watching particularly the increasing scope and momentum of its investigation from the end of the eighteenth century, I would like to note an advance in the science of moral duty, taken by the English at about that time.

When the American Revolution, from our point of view, is twice won, first in the mind and then in fact, we are left, on our side of the Atlantic, with the easy job of justifying our victory. The British, however, have to account for their defeat, and they do this by making a calculated step forward in ethical progress, moving on to a higher plateau or way station from where everybody was. Plumb says that they believed that the colonies were like children and that they, the British parent, had been terribly remiss in not taking proper care of them and guiding them and deserved to lose them. They had left things to the mercantile interests, but Christian responsibility implied a good deal more than that—precept and example, a firm hand—so they turned themselves half-circle towards the remaining empire they hadn't lost, towards India, whose relations had hitherto been cooly a matter of trade, and bore down upon this whole subcontinent with their new, righteous, paternalistic view of duty. Thus did the concept of the White Man's Burden get added to the White Man's sense of moral duty and represent an extension, a widening of the world-view. What seems in retrospect to be the incredible "moral vanity" of the Imperial mind was still, anyway, a higher plateau, a way station, in the progress of that science, and in the event contained sufficient contradiction to reward somebody from the psychological age for the effort of reading history. "There was better government, greater security of persons and property, than India had known for a century. Ignorant as he was of native ways and native customs, the British Raj was more just, and less extortionate, than his native counterpart. But the spiritual price India had to pay for these improvements was intolerably heavy. . . ."

It is the spiritual price that obsesses psychological man, and it is surely time that it did. The problem for older people toting, calculating, keeping books in the liberal tradition, is that to admit the spiritual price in the reckoning is to add an unencompassable dimension to our debts. To ask forgiveness for those debts, to forgive our debtors seems magnificently irrelevant. Forgive them? They want reparations, and they will dun us to the ground. The White Man's Burden now is to cope with the consequences of a white righteousness that bloated, in the era Victorian–Forever, our sense of moral duty as discerned by the Anglo-Saxon mind. "Search, search narrowly for that devil which may remain, search every corner . . . search with candles, make a curious search." That is the zeal with which our Puritan ancestors were exhorted to bear down on the enemy within, a curious search indeed. Later generations, passing through way stations, extended the search ever

outward, and it has after all been our American destiny to cul-
minate the process by making this curious search for enemies
the whole world over. You would think the progress of this
moral science would have no place left to go, the moon having
now been examined and found unimprovable. But our children, the revolutionaries, have rolled it on another half turn,
as though it were the rock of Sisyphus and it were their mission
to heave it onto dry level ground, with the bottom turned up
towards the sun: they make this curious search the whole world
over for *friends*.

By this laborious shove I wish, merely, to establish that if
I do see this new breed on a higher plateau, they are there
legitimately. They are not an irrational and unhistorical anom-
aly. It doesn't matter that there have always been others who
have strayed far out beyond the folk sense; it matters now that
they are arrived in peace, in numbers. Yesterday, in fact, they
were moving longitudinally in incredible numbers down our
own Elm Street, between two and three thousand of them,
honoring a national Moratorium, making that statement, and a
neighbor and I walked down Harrison Avenue to join them.
There wasn't a trace of incivility, and in fact that particular
moratorium may be an example of the most enormously *civil*
demonstration the word has embodied in human history.

The other afternoon, Maggie with me, I slowed the car to
let a few long-haired students of indeterminate sex cross the
street and had a little wave of acknowledgment from them.
Later, as it happened, I stopped for some aging women to go
by. No nod from them. "That's what I mean, mother," said
Maggie, "It seems to me our generation is always pleasant and
courteous and yours is always rude!" She had it the wrong way

around entirely, didn't she?

Today I am exalted by their demonstrated civility, but tomorrow that'll be the end of that. Something seeming small,
some "incivility" will be recorded in the *Times* and drain me of
my habitual sanguinity. And I'll take a dour look around,
knowing that incivility can be fatal to us all just because our
salvation depends upon the conventions of courtesy, and specifically the *mutuality* implicit in these conventions. To nod,
to wave, to shake hands, to smile at strangers for whom you
care not beans, all this civility is evidence of a kind of infrastructure for such extremely subtle necessary functions that
without it man could not have evolved, and building upon it
he might, he just might, skin past and on.

And the consequence of my being trained from childhood in
the science of moral duty is that it is habitual for me to behave
at least with civility in every interchange I have, and I acknowledge thereby, if tacitly, a minimum parity: we are both
human. Doubting my own senses sometimes, I nonetheless
assert by *my* courtesy that we are both human, and by this
fiction I deposit in him the necessity (as I see it) to respond
with courtesy: I construct the dialogue, I give him his part
(I nod, he nods,) his lines, ("Good Morning." "Good morning."). That is to say, I proceed on the sometimes unwarranted
assumption that he is up to the mark, is every bit a man, and
I use my acknowledgment of our human bond as leverage to
elicit his acknowledgment. That leverage in the convention of
little courtesies ("Thank you." "My pleasure, madam.") operates, when it does operate, in the larger courtesy of not littering our mutually trod-upon territory, this earth, and contains the power, I believe, by which we may devise conventions

for the supreme courtesy of not killing each other when we are crossed.

Brought thus far, these conventions become the "leverage of truth," Erikson's phrase for them in *Gandhi's Truth,* and this truth rests upon acknowledgment of our mutuality, which we need all to touch as we touch wood if we are to survive. *Gandhi's Truth* is not a biography of a strange and, to me, sometimes repellent saint. It is a most delicate, rich, presuming probe of the gestation and development of an ethic congruous with the needs of psychological man. (The first step is not to bring down with a crash the whole existing structure. The first step is to presume.)

I am still talking about the progress of a truth, the extension of caring and responsibility outward to encompass all mankind. The English mind extended its sense of caring and responsibility to improve the civil administration of India at an intolerably heavy spiritual price. It can be argued that Gandhi's great work in South Africa has come to less than nothing, and that he has left India less able, not more able, to govern herself. Yes, but it isn't my argument. It is the science of moral duty, how that is progressing, that absorbs me, and there's no question about Gandhi's contribution to that.

XVI A Lame Conclusion

But passing over the endless beautiful adaptations which we everywhere meet with, it may be asked how can the generally beneficent arrangement of the world be accounted for? Some writers indeed are so much impressed with the amount of suffering in the world, that they doubt if we look to all sentient beings, whether there is more of misery or of happiness;—whether the world as a whole is a good or a bad one. According to my judgment happiness decidedly prevails, though this would be very difficult to prove.

CHARLES DARWIN

All right. All right. I have about thirty more years to live through. Now What am I going to do? And will there be an appreciable change in my ways, in my roles, now that I am under my own direction? In my mind I catch Tony's cold glance at the life we lead, in a moment when he was hearing the grass grow and could not bear it. How loudly we wail for others, how well we take care of ourselves, said the glance. "You are an armchair liberal," I said to my father. "You are the great hypocrite generation," our children say to us.

I have discovered that I was born into a world in which a curtain had dropped between eye-witness and moral-witness, and, I acknowledge, one endured a painful dichotomy. A very breaking experience for many people it was, but to call us a great hypocrite generation, to single us out that way is too harsh. *"Petit hypocrite!"* Julian Sorel's father bawls after him. It's an epithet that echoes in my mind for its withering, shrinking effect. It sounds worse to be a little hypocrite than a big one, and worse still in French. I say I don't live with large discrepancies any more, but I shrug off many small ones. Would the young be more inclined to say that I don't live with the large hypocrisies any more—bully for me—just a lot of small ones? Perhaps I am unduly sensitive to seeming small on account of those mad saints on my mother's side who made the curious search for the small sins inside the self, those zealous proponents of the Contracting View, inspiration for small thinkers wherever. Have I not wriggled free of that heritage? And I hear my father's "You're talking nonsense," and his father's "She's a damn fool." When I was growing up I sometimes would try to tell my father about an injustice I had unearthed, and he would tell me I was talking nonsense, but I wasn't. Sometimes I tell myself I'm a damn fool, and I am.

I have written the story of the opening up of me. It seems an abrupt event, but it must have been welling through the 60s. It's all in my mind. However, no longer is it a test of my loyalty, my literacy, my maternity to brush away evidence that doesn't fit the neatly trimmed world view of my childhood. I am willing to let appalling insights, intractable facts, ugly, beautiful, irreversible, unamendable, hopeless, and, above all, contradictory bits of knowledge that are in infinite supply, let all that be deposited on the table, above board, along with timeless truths, timeless beauties. It makes a puzzle that *can't* be put together. How tormenting and how unfair for old buffs. But I? I'm not really rattled. I'm not really often rattled. That is the Act of Enablement the young have performed for me.

To be *alone* and hear the squirrel's heart beat and the grass grow, to bear the pain and poignancy of life in such detail, well, it is true I could not bear much of it. But I am not alone with these facts that I know and can't unknow in this psychological age. I have the company of the new breed, evolved in surprising and unlooked-for numbers, some living in this very house, a great fellowship who amazingly can take it all in.

Given that I am now thus enabled, it might be asked may the world expect to be grateful for my new wide vision, and by what signs shall it know me? My hair is short and my dress modest. Julie says that Me, the liberated woman, the relaxed, permissive latitudinarian Now-Mother, is indistinguishable from the pre-revolutionary close-minded, arbitrary Matriarch she's owned since birth. You can't tell by my outward signs, I guess. It's all in my mind.

I quoted earlier this cry from Bernard Bailyn's book, "When tyranny is abroad, submission is a crime!" the cry that testified to the revolution's being completed in the colonial mind before 1776. Then it was the cry of the undernation. Now it is the cry of the underperson. People won't submit to the tyranny of past institutions. They won't submit to the hierarchical rule, particularly if they are at the bottom end of the stairs. If they're black, they won't agree to be racially inferior; if they're women, they won't agree to be sexually inferior; if they're not Americans, they won't agree to be sorry about it; if they're young, they won't agree they are less wise. It is an anarchic situation. Frightening numbers of people now see that personal freedom might really be within their grasp, and they will let everything else fall by the wayside, let everything else be sacrificed, desecrated, madly undervalued. I am in an anguish over the tearing down of our beautiful culture, and I would do anything to defend and preserve it, anything except yield my personal freedom, this new sense of autonomy. I recognize their stake, and it stays my hand.

I had no more than finished this thesis that the revolutions had been completed than there burst upon me the women's liberation movement. "But you *are* liberated." I protest. "It's just a matter now of tidying up the legislative ends, of abortion reform, and equal pay" (—which puts me in the position of saying that how the law treats you, how society regards you, do not affect the way you see yourself; that is clearly untrue).

"No," they say. "The really radical revolution is yet to begin. We must find an alternative to the nuclear family. Sexual differences are culturally determined, and we must devise new child-rearing practices to eradicate them, and to begin with a wife must demand equal time as the bread-winner, and her husband must put in equal time with the baby-tending and dish-washing." She will not wash dishes nor yet feed the swine, nor sit on a cushion and sew a fine seam, if he doesn't.

I see this new wild women's thrust towards a personal autonomy I had already endowed them with, and I think, as to the sexual revolution, I may have jumped the gun. I believe in their politics but I don't believe in their "science," that *all* sexual differences are culturally determined, and when I listen to their indictment against that joyless, beaten, condemned inferior who dumbly accepts the housewife's duty, my head hanging at the sad shame of it all, why, the next thing that I hear is Beatrice Lillie singing "There are Fairies at the Bottom of My Garden," trilling in a sneaky way to an excrutiating triumph.

"The Queen—now can you guess who that could be?
She's a little girl by day, but at night she steals
away—
Well—IT'S MEEEEE!"

Well, it's me. I could not for the moment recognize my younger self in their description of the dreary wife/mother, so rich, so sweet, so joyful are my screened memories. It was indeed the part of my life that wasn't fair, wasn't equal. It was nonpareil. My revolution isn't an overthrow of the femaleness of women, but of their lesserness. Black is beautiful, women are beautiful, men are beautiful—I like that. I like the potential peerlessness of everybody, that each one of us is unique, unprecedented, unrepeatable. I believe woman is as fully human as man, a revolutionary view, and that is the *fait accompli* that I mean.

Equal fails to define the relationship of woman to man and when somebody said to me recently, "Mrs. Seton, you enjoy being a woman so much, do you think she is equal?" I was brought low by the phrasing and answered, "Yes, we are equal. We are all up here together and the view is devastating, despairful." It is a despairful view and I have about thirty more years to look at it, and I remember that there is substantial scientific opinion that claims all life, all humanity, has only thirty more years, using the nest-fouling scale. So we'll go together. It breaks my heart. It seems that the Last Judgment in the trial of man is being announced and runs against us. ("Seems, madam! Nay it is: I know not 'seems' ").

My despair is easily accounted for.

But my exhilaration?

Well, sometimes I think it is a matter of temperament, and behind that, a matter of chemistry. Darwin thought happiness decidedly prevailed, and he, after all, not only suffered his long life through with debilitating physical ailments, but he had, laid out perpetually before him, the evidence of suffering through an extent of time never before encompassed by man's mind. "That there is much suffering in the world no one disputes," he writes in his autobiography. "Some have attempted to explain this in reference to man by imagining that it serves for his moral improvement. But the number of men in the world is as nothing compared with that of all other sentient beings, and these often suffer greatly without any moral improvement." All that suffering *without* moral improvement, and still he concludes that the world is a good one.

It is temperament, chemistry, that has me exult over evidence that man's expanding intellectual grasp, combined with an increasing ethical sophistication, is evolving with a rapidity that brings him at least within crying distance of the forces that will destroy him. I am capable of being awestruck by the idea of evolution, by the order, the ubiquity, the incessance of it on the one hand, and by the chance and variation of it on the other. I see the new breed arrived just possibly in time as its great triumph.

I live without God but not without comfort: which I derive from the belief that the humanity of humanity is fit enough to survive the struggle for existence alongside the murderous passions, and is as tenacious. People look at the 60s and see a great closing, hear the tolling of the bell. I see a great opening.

I see the young by the millions standing on top of this decade casting down illusions with a fierce, righteous ruthlessness like a gaunt medieval Christ casting down devils. They don't give me hope for the future, but they do give me this sense of personal worth for the present.